CARDBOARD CITY

Katarina Jovanovic

CARDBOARD CITY

TRADEWIND BOOKS
Vancouver • London

To my youngest child, Dev—KJ

ACKNOWLEDGEMENTS

I appreciate the courage of Michael Katz and Carol Frank to publish *Cardboard City*, a book dealing with sensitive issues which tells a story about a people little known in Canada.

Thank you to my daughter Ljudmila Petrovic—the first person with whom I discussed my idea for this book and its storyline, and who helped me edit its first draft.

• • •

The publisher thanks Slobodan Stankovic for reading the manuscript and kindly offering his editorial advice.

The publisher would also like to thank Ana Belen Martin Sevillano, Associate Professor in the Department of Literature and Languages, Université de Montréal, for her editorial advice.

Finally, the publisher wishes to also thank Delia Radu of the BBC for reading the book and sharing her thoughts.

In 2005. Delia Radu made a series of 10 radio programs for the BBC to commemorate a '*Decade of Roma Inclusion*' launched by the World Bank, the United Nations, and the Council of Europe. In 2015 Delia travelled to Romania and Slovakia for a report on the BBC World Service on whether "the Decade" kept its promise.

CONTENTS

In May 2009, the City of Belgrade displaced Cardboard City, an informal settlement of nearly 1000 people— mostly Romani—situated below the Gazela Bridge across from the Hyatt and Intercontinental Hotels. But *Cardboard City* is not just about this settlement—nor is it a story only about Romani people. These events could be about marginalized and impoverished people anywhere in the world. It could take place in the suburbs of Rome, in the favelas of Sao Paolo, in Dharavi in Mumbai, in the Downtown Eastside of Vancouver—or in refugee camps anywhere around the world.

*We are all wanderers on this earth; our hearts are
full of wonder and our souls are full of dreams.*

ROMANI PROVERB

CHAPTER 1

Nikola

RIKA MET NIKOLA AT THE SUMMER FAIR. The field was filled with Romani tents, trucks and trailers. People were busily setting up a new fairground for the summer. Travelling artists from different parts of the country had already arrived—musicians and fortune-tellers. There were also merry-go-rounds, ponies, games, and vendors of candies and corn cakes.

Rika had arrived at the fairground with his small trumpet quartet. When his band started playing, Rika noticed two Romani boys in the audience entirely immersed in the music—one with a glass eye and a skinny one who seemed to be on the verge of tears. While they performed *Carnival in Paris*, the skinny boy held his hands out to form a trumpet. His fingers moved its imaginary keys. His cheeks bulged out and his throat hummed along with the music.

"Hey boy, you play the trumpet. Know the song?" one of the trumpet players shouted at Nikola.

"I know it very well. I played it many times," the boy shouted back. "I can play it in my mind even without a trumpet." He shivered with excitement.

"In your mind? That must be good music!"

Everyone laughed. The boy got up and fled in tears.

When the band finished playing, Rika packed up his trumpet and approached the boy sitting with his friend in the shade of an oak tree. He was blowing his nose and his eyes were red from crying.

"So you know how to play the trumpet," Rika said, sitting down next to him.

"A little."

"Why don't you show me what you know?" he said, handing his trumpet to Nikola.

The boy lifted Rika's trumpet to his lips. He played with his eyes closed.

When the song was over, Rika nodded enthusiastically.

He looked at Nikola in disbelief. "You play very well! Where did you learn that? I have never heard a boy your age play with such feeling. Who taught you?"

"My grandfather, but he died last year. Then my neighbour's brother came to see his relatives in Cardboard City. He taught me what I know, but he returned home to another town. I used to practice on my grandfather's trumpet, but my sister, Saida, took it with her when she ran away from home."

"What else do you know?"

Nikola played. Rika was now genuinely excited.

"What's your name?"

"Nikola. And this is my friend Spoon."

"Nikola, I'm Rika." They shook hands.

"Tomorrow morning we are packing up and going to Guča where there's a big brass festival. Almira, my girlfriend, will be with me. There are brass bands playing everywhere there."

"Oh, my grandfather went there all the time."

As Rika glanced at his watch and got up to leave, Nikola said, "Maybe I can help you in Guča, if you give me a ride there."

"Well, sure, but you need to ask your parents."

"I live with Baba, my grandmother," he said. "I'll ask her for permission. Where can I find you tomorrow morning?"

"Come with me, and I'll show you where I live."

Rika's trailer looked small and wretched from the outside, but it was spacious inside, divided into several areas. One area was the kitchen—food boxes, eggs, pots with food, plates and spoons were all scattered in a corner. A slim young woman stood by the stove stirring the pot.

"Almira, we have a visitor. This is Nikola. He might go with us to Guča tomorrow. Do you have an extra plate for our guest?"

Three small stools were arranged around the food and the dishes. Almira pointed at one and got busy filling up the tin plate with hot yellow *kachamak*—corn porridge—which she sprinkled with red paprika and decorated on top with a generous spoonful of creamy *kaymak*.

She placed the plate and the spoon in front of Nikola.

"*Manjaj!* Eat up!"

Almira had stepped out of the trailer, and when she returned, Nikola was licking the melted kaymak off the plate. She handed him a white shirt and pants. "Here, I got these from the tailor. He gave them to me for free. I think that they might fit you.

"You sure were hungry!" She laughed, flashing a crown of beautiful white teeth. "You cleaned the plate. So you like my cooking? And that was only kachamak. Wait until you try my stuffed cabbage. You will eat the skin off your fingers. Ask your parents if you can come with us to Guča. We leave early tomorrow."

Not all men are like trees; some must
travel and cannot keep still
ROMANI PROVERB

CHAPTER 2

Spoon

WHEN HE LEFT RIKA'S TRAILER, Nikola wandered back to the fair not knowing what to do.

What now? he thought.

Asking Baba was out of the question. She would never let him go. Not at this time, not when his sister, Saida, was missing, not when everybody was looking for her. He thought about their hut, Saida's empty bed in the morning, Baba weeping.

He could ask someone to pretend to be his mother or father, but that person would want a bribe, and he didn't have any money. The only option was to go to Guča hiding in someone's truck.

Walking around and listening to people's conversations might lead him to discover who was going to Guča.

"The big merry-go-round launches to outer space!" a heavy-set Romani man announced to the crowd. He pushed the button and started the merry-go-round. It circled around with children giggling and waving their arms in the air.

Nikola got dizzy from watching.

A girl with long dark pigtails came out of a tent to invite the audience in. "Come and see the snake-woman: half woman, half snake! Her poor mother, she was hoping to have a healthy daughter and look what happened instead! Come and meet the woman inside a snake's body. I guarantee you've never seen anything like it before. Only one dinar per ticket."

Nikola *had* to see the snake-woman. He crawled underneath the tent. And there she was—a woman in a tight plastic snake costume sitting in a glass box.

The girl with long pigtails ushered the spectators closer to the box and pointed at the woman's costumed body. "Come a bit closer. It's safe—she won't hurt anyone. Look at the snake-woman. Her name is Mimi. Mimi, show these people your snake body!"

The woman in the box rubbed her plastic tail with her hands.

"Mimi, wash your face with soap."

Mimi pretended that she was washing her face.

"Mimi, greet the audience."

Mimi waved with her tail. That was the end of the show. Nikola crawled out.

Further down, they were just starting a motorcycle show.

"Little Zoran and little Zora, brother and sister, on the wall of death riding motorcycles. The first time in Europe! Never seen before in the world, only once in Australia."

Nikola couldn't waste any more time. He nervously approached the girl with pigtails. "Do you know anybody who is going to Guča tomorrow?"

"To Guča? Let me think . . . Rika the musician is going to Guča."

"Do you know anybody else?"

"Why are you asking? Will you buy me an ice cream?"

"I have no money," Nikola said. "I am looking for somebody to take me there. Or to hide in somebody's truck."

"I'll find out for you."

She came back soon.

"You can try the watermelon truck," the girl whispered in his ear. "They are just packing up to leave. When they cover the truck, you can just jump in. I'll distract them, while you climb in."

"You are so nice. What can I do for you in return?"

"You can kiss me," the girl said shyly. "I need practice kissing."

"I've never kissed a girl."

"Don't worry. Just be quick or you will miss the truck for Guča."

Nikola stepped up to the girl and touched her hand.

"Over here," she said, taking his hand and pulling him behind one of the tents.

Nikola kissed her on the left cheek.

"Are you kidding me? I meant a real kiss, mouth to mouth."

"I don't know how to do it."

"Just close your eyes."

The girl's mouth was sweet and sticky.

She probably ate cotton candy just a minute ago, he thought.

When he opened his eyes, the girl was smiling. "That was a good kiss! Now hurry, the trucks are leaving. I'll go and stop them while you jump in."

Nikola jumped into one of the trucks and hid under the canvas. But just when he thought that his plan was working, the truck stopped. He heard voices outside and then an enormous hairy hand grabbed him by the sleeve and pulled him out.

"You think you are so smart, running away from home and hiding in my truck. Out!"

Nikola felt a kick in his backside as he jumped out. Then the truck pulled off down the dusty road, leaving him behind.

Crestfallen, he walked back to the fairground.

It was getting late and most of the other trucks and trailers had already packed up. The girl with pigtails was still there licking another cotton candy.

He found Spoon asleep by the river.

• • •

Spoon had a glass eye that twinkled in the dark, making it easy to recognise him at night—it shone like a lighthouse. When he wanted to focus on an object, he had to turn his entire body toward it. He also had a speech impediment. To communicate, Spoon and Nikola used a special code that only the two of them understood. For example, touching his glass eye with one finger meant *a shop window*, rubbing his stomach meant *we have to work all day with no food*, two hands around his neck meant *watch out, the cops are around*, and covering an eye with one palm meant *you are my friend through thick and thin*.

• • •

"Everybody thinks I'm stupid, but I'm not. That's my best kept secret," Spoon had confided to Nikola one day.

Spoon grew up in his grandfather's cottage in a small village in Serbia. The cottage had been given to his grandfather as a gift from a man whose life his grandpa had saved during the war. Even though his father drank away all the money his mother had earned fortune-telling, washing laundry and selling homemade honey cookies, the family managed to get by. After Spoon's grandpa died, Spoon's mother packed all their belongings and went to Belgrade, thinking she could find a place to live there. But she soon found out she couldn't afford anything. Luckily, one day a Romani woman she met at the market told her about Cardboard City. People there helped her build an improvised hut to live in, and a couple of months after they settled in Cardboard City, Spoon's father joined them. When Spoon was six, his father, who was rarely sober, got angry with him while they were eating a bean soup. He splashed him on the face with a spoon full of beans. From then on, Spoon hated bean soup and was afraid of spoons. The other children teased him for that and started calling him Spoon. Soon, nobody, not even his mother, remembered his real name anymore. Everybody knew him as Spoon.

Spoon had become a hero of Cardboard City a few years previously, after the celebration of the Feast of Saint Nicholas. After an all-day community feast of fish, cabbage rolls, *pogačica*, bulghur wheat, beer and wine, everyone fell asleep early in the evening—except for Spoon.

Spoon stayed up late that night, keeping an eye on the money left beneath the icon of Saint Nicholas. He thought that it would be easy to take some of it, after everyone was fast asleep, to buy glasses. It was Spoon's dream to wear glasses, which he thought might help him see more clearly.

He stayed awake until three o'clock in the morning when the last of the drinkers had fallen asleep. But the moment he touched the icon, he heard a crackling of wood and dry leaves and smelled a fire. He spotted a pail of water and emptied it onto the fire—but the fire wouldn't go out. He tried to shout for help, but was paralyzed with fear, so he grabbed an empty tin pail and created such a clamorous sound that all the stray dogs barked at once. At last awakened, the Romani men and women came running out.

Alarmed by the fire, they ran to find water, shouting and waking everyone up. That night witnessed the biggest fire in the history of Cardboard City. It took hours to put it out. Fire trucks had to come from the heart of the city to deal with the flames. Luckily, nobody was hurt. From then on, everybody talked about how brave Spoon was, and Spoon never admitted what had really happened that night.

● ● ●

Nikola shook Spoon to wake him up.

"I have to get to Guča, and you need to help me. We have to find somebody who will pretend to be from my family and give that trumpet player Rika permission to take me to Guča."

"Who would do that? Especially now that everyone is searching for Saida. What if she is dead?"

"She's not dead. She just ran away from home. I have to get to the trumpet festival in Guča tomorrow. I can't go later, it'll be over. Get it? Are you going to help me?"

"No," Spoon answered.

It was dark out and most of the stalls in the fairground were closing.

So they made their way home.

Nikola found Baba sitting alone by the stove, wrapped in a woollen shawl. Leaning forward, with her eyebrows knitted together in a frown, she appeared to him smaller and older.

The Decision

"**B**ABA?"

"Yes, my Nikolche."

"Baba, I have something to tell you." He heard his own voice in the dark silence of the hut. "Otherwise, the stone in my heart will grow bigger, and it'll explode."

Baba pulled a piece of apple out of her apron pocket. She broke up a walnut with her feet, rubbed it against her blouse and handed the pieces to Nikola.

"What is it, my darling?"

Never before had Nikola heard Baba's voice being that gentle. He started telling her about his dreams of becoming a trumpet player. He told her about Rika, Almira and their plan to take him with them to the trumpet festival in Guča. And he told her about Bosco, their neighbour's brother from another town, the man who was his trumpet teacher. How they bonded through trumpet music. How one night, the sound of a trumpet had caught his attention. The music was so much like Deda's— Grandfather's. Nikola thought that Deda was the only one who played like that. It was powerful and then gentle and mellow.

In the silence of the night, all he could hear was his own whispering voice, as he told Baba his story.

"So I followed the sound to a bench by the river. A Romani man was sitting there, playing the trumpet, deep in his music. I sat quietly close by, listening. When the piece was finished, the man took off his hat and started wiping his sweaty face with a handkerchief. He didn't see me, or at least he pretended not to."

• • •

"Good playing!" I said.

The man did not seem at all surprised to hear my voice from out of the darkness.

"You like it?"

"Very much."

"What is your name?"

"Nikola."

"How old are you?"

"Thirteen."

"Do you play an instrument yourself?"

"My grandfather did, before he died. He taught me some songs. He sometimes allowed me to play his trumpet—but only on special occasions, because the trumpet meant so much to him. He said that it's the most precious of all our possessions."

The man laughed.

"Do you have brothers and sisters?"

"I have an older sister, Saida. She is the prettiest and proudest girl in our neighbourhood. She rejects all the boys—she says she wants to make something out of her life. I don't know what she means by that. Baba gets angry with her sometimes. They fight all the time."

"I know. I have a family too. That's why I am here in the city—to see them. They live in Cardboard City like you. You like music, aah? Music is *baht*! Brings good luck!"

"I would like to play the trumpet myself. I often dream that I am playing the trumpet."

"If such a young child dreams of playing an instrument, it means that he is a born musician."

"My grandfather once went to Guča and took part in the brass trumpet competition. When he played, everybody around the fire cried. Even the men. They say that his music shook the soul."

"Do you want to learn how to play well?"

"Like you?"

"Maybe even better than me."

"Well, yes!"

"Then I can teach you."

"How much money would you ask for?"

"I will teach you for free. Can you find this bench again tomorrow?"

"I think so."

"Then I will wait for you tomorrow just before sunset, and we'll start learning."

When Nikola's story came to the part where he took Grandfather's trumpet to the bench by the river, Baba's lips trembled, but she didn't say anything.

"Are you ready for the lesson?" the man asked Nikola.

Nikola nodded.

"To begin with, understand that our lips are the most important part of our body if we play an instrument like the trumpet."

The man pointed at the small opening on the instrument.

"This is called a mouthpiece. In this trumpet, it is cupped, but it can have other shapes as well. You get the right sound by placing your mouth on this cup here—put your lips here and smile . . . now blow. That's the correct position for trumpet playing. Now, let's practice a bit with your tongue."

Nikola had started picking up his grandfather's trumpet when he was little. He had watched his grandfather blowing, pressing the buttons, and making music. He learned how to hold the trumpet like a real musician by watching Deda's band while they played. Now Bosco showed him that to play you needed proper training. The right sound did not come out of the trumpet easily—it required skill.

At the end of summer Bosco said, "Today I want to teach you to play one long and difficult song. Do you know what song you want to learn first?"

" 'Carnival in Paris'!" blurted Nikola without having to think twice. "My grandfather used to play that song to cheer people up."

"Do you know where Paris is?" asked Bosco.

"I have no idea, but I always think about sausages when I hear the song."

Bosco laughed. "Maybe because there's a kind of sausage called Parisian sausage. Paris is the capital of France, much like Belgrade is the capital of Serbia—just bigger and more beautiful. The city of the Eiffel Tower."

The man pulled out his cellphone and showed Nikola pictures of Paris. "One day maybe, you can go there and play your trumpet. You never know!"

"Maybe one day."

"Anyway," the man continued, "it's very important for you to visualize the story the music is telling you. Every song tells a story. You can't play music well if you don't know what the story behind it is."

The next evening, the man brought Nikola several pictures of Paris. "You can keep one for yourself."

That night, Nikola hung a picture of the Eiffel Tower on the wall by his bed, attaching it with chewing gum.

It felt lonely when Bosco left town, but Nikola continued to practice on his grandfather's trumpet every evening. When winter came and rain began to drip through a hole in the ceiling, Nikola covered the picture with a clear plastic bag to protect it.

Every night, he would fall asleep, looking at that cold iron tower that reached all the way to the sky.

• • •

Baba listened to his story in silence.

"That man will never return," she said shaking her head.

"How do you know?" asked Nikola surprised

"I know people. But you ought to be grateful to him for the rest of your life. He gave you so much. Let's pray for him."

So, they prayed together for the man who had taught Nikola to play the trumpet.

When they lifted their heads after prayers, Baba said, "So, let's hear you play. I will borrow a trumpet from our neighbour."

She went to the hut of their neighbour, another trumpet player.

When his grandmother returned, she passed the trumpet to Nikola.

"What do you want me to play, Baba?"

"A real trumpet player doesn't ask, he feels."

Baba was waiting for him to start.

Nikola closed his eyes, and the music came. He played one song, and then played it again. He didn't dare look at his grandmother when he stopped playing. He nervously glanced at her through the broken mirror. Baba was wiping away tears. When he turned toward her, she didn't say anything.

There was a sudden knock at the hut, and a tiny woman with bony hands came in. She was dressed in a brown vinyl raincoat and wore a pungent perfume. She was a frequent visitor to his grandmother's house.

Baba was a fortune-teller—she employed a crystal ball, beans, egg white, coffee beans, tea leaves, bones and playing cards. Romani fortune-tellers such as Baba seldom told the future to her fellow Roma; this they mostly did for a *gadjo*, a non-Romani person.

"You must read to me, Ramina," said the woman. "I had a bad dream."

"There is no such thing as a bad dream," said Baba, in a calm voice. "All dreams are good. Dreams—they guide us in life. What's bad is not having dreams at all. Wait, I'll make you some coffee."

"Thank you, Ramina, thank you so much. God sees your goodness."

"So, what was the dream?" interrupted Baba.

The woman whispered her dream. Ramina nodded.

"I will look in your coffee cup," she said.

Baba made a strong thick Turkish coffee and filled two small cups. They drank up. The woman shook her cup vigorously and turned it upside down on a piece of paper. Baba touched the bottom of the cup. She carefully observed the shapes in the grinds of coffee, whispered some words and quickly turned over the cup. She rotated it with two fingers analysing its content. Baba's forefinger was bigger and fatter than her other fingers; she used that finger for coffee reading. She placed it on the inside of the cup and twisted it clockwise.

"Lots of white here," Baba said thoughtfully. "You know the white spots in the coffee cup are good fortune, while the black coffee grounds are bad."

"Good," said the woman, sounding relieved.

"A big apple," Baba continued. "Somebody finishing school."

The woman gazed at the coffee cup. "Must be my son. That means that he will finish this year."

"He will, he will. I can see that," said Baba, nodding. "You have a very small bird flying toward you. A postcard or a letter, nothing big. A dog with wide eyes. A very loyal friend in the family. Could be a relative. It's all good."

Baba handed the coffee cup back to the woman. The woman licked her thumb and pressed hard on the bottom. That was the final stage of coffee reading—making a print in the coffee sediment and making a wish.

"The family is stable. I don't see any trouble here."

"Thank God," sighed the woman, crossing herself.

"I see good fortune coming to you, but it is still unclear from where it will come. There is a dark-haired man with a moustache knocking on your door, but you are not at home."

"What does that mean, Ramina? Is he bringing something important? What should I do? Not leave home until he comes?"

"I don't know. It is hard to say. I see a dark-haired man at your door. It can be somebody official—police or insurance. Can be anybody, it is too early to say. Maybe if you come tomorrow as well, the shapes will be clearer?"

"I will come, for sure, I will come. Thank you, Ramina."

The woman put the money in his grandmother's pocket and left. Even though Baba believed that it was insulting to take money for advice, it was well-known that her services were not free. So money would be slid into her pocket.

Nikola went behind the curtain and peered into the woman's cup. He did not see anything there except the coffee grounds.

"Baba," he asked. "Where is the dark-haired man here? Where is the small bird? I cannot see an apple either. I don't see anything like that in the cup."

"You can't see because you are not a fortune-teller," Baba said, putting the cups away.

Another woman entered the kitchen. "I have only enough money for a short fortune-telling," she said.

She sat down and Baba shuffled, then flipped over the cards.

"Ace of Hearts. Good. Home and love. Pleasant news. Love letter. Watch out for gossip."

Baba dropped the cards and lit up a cigarette. "I don't want to say any more. You said you had the money only for a quick fortune-telling."

The woman slid a note into Baba's pocket. Her face shone in expectation. "Ramina, my husband has been away for three days. I don't know what to do. Maybe something happened to him, or maybe he is with another woman. Maybe he left me. Can you see that in your cards?"

"I can see everything in my cards. I am the best fortune-teller in this area. Nobody ever complained about my services."

The woman wiped her eyes with a pink handkerchief. "I want to know if he is alive or dead. Is he cheating on me or did something happen to him? I am so worried, Ramina. I haven't slept for two days."

Baba laid out the cards. Three rows of seven cards, from left to right. The bottom represented the future. She was going to open that one first. The woman sat with her eyes glued on the cards.

If Baba told her bad news and it actually happened, she might say Baba was a witch. If she lied, the woman would say she had been conned and tell her friends that she was a con artist.

"Open the cards please," the woman whispered.

Baba did. "Ten of spades: sorrow, loss of freedom, sad journey." The woman's face was white and the black sacs underneath her eyes trembled in expectation.

How can I break the bad news to her? Baba thought. "I made a mistake. And now it is too late to do it again. I have work to do."

"I am not paying for this!" the woman said.

"Such is life," Baba said calmly.

The woman left, weeping.

Baba was tired and ill. There were only two souls she cared for, Nikola and Saida.

When she finished, she put away the cards and went to return the trumpet to her neighbour.

Nikola stayed in the kitchen waiting for her to come back. He was anxious to hear what Baba thought about his music. To kill time, he lay down and looked at the picture of Paris, which was still hanging next to his bed. That's how he fell asleep.

Baba woke him up early the next mroning.

"Get ready!" she said, wrapping a slice of bread and garlic in her scarf. "Garlic is for luck. Bread is for the journey."

"Where are we going?"

"I am not going anywhere. You are going to Guča. I am taking you to that man you met in the fairground. If I find that he is honest, you can go with him to Guča."

"But Baba, I was thinking last night that I can't go—you need me here."

"I don't need you here."

"What am I going to do in Guča?"

"Play the trumpet."

"Nobody will listen to me."

"There is always somebody who listens. You need to go. We Roma say: *Not all men are like trees; some must travel and cannot keep still.*"

CHAPTER 4

The Encounter

ALMIRA BROKE THE WATERMELON and cut it into red and juicy slices. Could there be anything better? A slice was gone in a couple of bites and then, her favourite part—throw it over the fence! Her arm stretched high as she aimed into the horizon. A sudden shout on the other side of the fence made her shiver and move away from the fence—the watermelon rind had hit somebody.

Almira shifted her focus to the trip. In less than an hour they would be on their way to Guča, a busy town pulsing with life, especially during the trumpet festival when people danced all night.

Almira stretched again and threw another watermelon rind over the fence. She felt perfectly at peace with the world, just like she did after having a glass of fresh, cold stream water. She was twenty-one and this would be her first trip to Guča without her father, a well-known trumpeter, who had performed at all the important music festivals in Serbia. After Almira's mother had passed away, she was the only one to accompany her father to the festival. After her mother's early death, her father worked nights playing in restaurants and slept in the morning. Almira did all the cooking, cleaning and taking care of her younger siblings. When all the housework was done and the younger children were asleep, Almira liked to sit at the kitchen table and make jewelry. She would sell it at the Sunday market. That's how she met Rika.

"Good morning." A short bony Romani woman stood there calmly holding a boy's hand. He wore a white shirt and an embroidered brown vest. It was the boy who had come the day before, the one Rika promised to take to Guča with his parents' permission. *Rika said the boy had a talent for music.* The woman had dark angry eyes and her eyebrows were close together. She had deep wrinkles all over her rough, dark brown skin. The boy stood still beside her, his pale sad eyes downcast.

The woman rubbed her neck and pulled a watermelon seed out of her shirt.

"If I catch that devil who threw the watermelon rind over the fence! Nowadays you can't even walk in the fields without being hurt. I came to see the man whose name is Rika about taking my grandson to the trumpet festival in Guča. Isn't that his name, Nikolche?"

She turned to the boy, and he nodded.

Almira worried that the woman might realize that she was the one who had thrown the watermelon rind over the fence. She looked around the trailer—the knife and the tray were still there, soaked in red juice and littered with watermelon seeds.

Almira finally spoke up. "Who should I say is looking for him?"

"Ramina from Cardboard City. Everyone calls me Baba, and

you can call me that too. The boy's name is Nikola."

"Wait here. Rika will be back right away. I will get some cold water for Nikola and make coffee for you."

CHAPTER 5

The Gambling

R IKA'S LEAN FINGERS STRETCHED like miniature dancers on a stage, moving the match boxes at a dizzying speed. Then he stopped abruptly and gave the impression that the metal ball was under a particular match box. To make it even more obvious for everyone watching, he rested his thumb on it.

"Now, who wants to bet? Just guess where the ball is."

Rika glanced at his audience: easy money this time—an elderly gentleman, a young couple and a teenager who smelled of marijuana. If they all bet, he would earn thirty dinars.

His thumb was on the match box. "I made it too easy. Chip in ten dinars each. If you all bet on the same one and win, you all share the money. Here are thirty dinars from me."

He pulled out a thirty dinar note. They chipped in and pointed at the match box with Rika's thumb on it.

This was his moment. It always brought him a unique pleasure when he knew before the others that he would win. He read hope, triumph and excitement on their faces. But it would all vanish in the moment they found out they had guessed wrong.

Rika was a master of trickery, a king of fraud. He was born with a rare ability—to deceive. He thought of himself as a trickster. Rika chose when to trick and whom to trick. The other thing he took pride in was his generosity and kindness. He wouldn't do any harm if he didn't have to. Sometimes he even felt sorry for his victims, those who were losing the game, and he changed the boxes quickly to allow them to win. Rika could do that—he could roll the ball from under one match box to under another without anybody being aware of it. *Fools*, he thought. *Don't gamble with me.* He could read contempt in their eyes, but he always outsmarted a punter.

Here it is . . . he gently pushed the foil ball from under one box to under another. Then he lifted the match box that had his thumb on it. Empty. He quickly put the money in his pocket and wrapped up the game in a handkerchief. The teenager left the place. The elderly gentleman still stood there in disbelief.

The couple argued. "I told you!" the girl shouted angrily to her boyfriend. "You can't win this game. They trick you every time! He moved the ball." They disappeared into the crowd.

Rika's shirt was damp. The humidity by the river in August was unbearable. *What idiots! Easy money*, he thought. He was satisfied with himself.

While he was heading to the trailer, he reflected on how sad the boy seemed. But he was a good trumpet player. A natural. He could be a big help on their trip. Rika drank some water from the stream. It was cold and refreshed him completely. He would buy a necklace for Almira.

They would take the boy to Guča, if the boy got permission. He, Rika, was a first-class trickster, a champion, with a big heart. He picked up his trumpet and dashed back to the trailer.

CHAPTER 6

The Permission

NIKOLA'S GRANDMOTHER WAS SITTING on a rock next to the trailer. The boy stood beside her.

"Somebody visiting us?" Rika's voice thundered as he walked up. Almira came out with coffee and water.

The woman took a loud sip from the coffee cup. "It's about my grandson," she explained, gently touching Nikola's hand. "He plays trumpet and wants to go to Guča."

"Of course, I know him," Rika said—Rika wasn't Rom, but he grew up with Romani people, understood the boy's grandmother and knew how to talk to her. "He came yesterday, and I promised to take him there if his parents gave permission. I gather that you are in charge of him. Will you give your permission?"

"First, I need to see if I can trust you. This boy is everything I have in the world. His sister ran away. Now I only have him. He is a good boy. Sensitive. He cries easily. I am worried something might happen to him. I can't let him go just like that."

Nikola didn't like to hear that he cried easily, but he was glad that Baba cared about him.

"That's natural. What do you need to know?"

"Are you from here?"

"Yes, but we travel in summer."

"What do you do when you travel?"

"We sell watermelons, but I mainly play trumpet in festivals, weddings and funerals."

"And who is this young woman? Is she your wife?"

"We work together. As for your grandson, I will protect him like my own son. Do you want some watermelon?" He cut a slice for himself, chewed it up in two bites and threw the rind over the fence.

Baba watched him closely.

"Where will he sleep?" she finally asked.

"Inside the trailer, like us," said Rika, pointing with his head.

"Will you bring him right back home?"

"Sure. We'll bring him straight home."

"Do you need any money for the boy's food?"

"You can give him some if you like. Otherwise, he can always get a bowl of whatever we are having in the pot."

"He really wants to go."

"No worries," said Rika looking at Nikola. "We'll take care of him."

"I give my permission then," Baba said finally, letting Nikola's hand go. She pulled a banknote from inside her blouse and stuck it in Nikola's pocket. Then she kissed him on the forehead, spat on the ground a couple of times to protect him from bad spirits, and left. Nikola watched Baba's limping figure as it disappeared behind the fence.

"Time to get ready and go," Rika said.

They watched the boy climb up the trailer stairs as they collected up all the clutter around the trailer.

CHAPTER 1

A strange boy—fragile and yet so determined, Almira thought.

"He has a gift for playing the trumpet," Rika said as the boy disappeared into the truck.

CHAPTER 7

The Trip

WHILE THEY WERE DRIVING TO GUČA, Rika let Nikola sit beside him on the front seat. They passed farmhouses, corn and wheat fields. The road was bumpy, and Nikola choked on the dust and truck diesel fumes. He felt sick to his stomach, unsure of whether his sickness came from hunger or car fumes. For the first time in his life, Nikola rode in a truck, wore a shirt and a vest, entered a trailer, and saw the hills. In the city, there were buildings and houses, cars and buses and street cars. There were no hills and mountains.

Along the way they passed sheep and horses grazing in fields. There were some horses in Nikola's settlements, but no sheep. "We keep ducks and chickens," Nikola said, breaking the silence. "Baba treats them like family; they eat the same food as we do. Sometimes they sleep on Baba's lap and drink from her mug."

"Pets?" Rika asked.

"No. At Christmas and Easter, Baba chooses one, prays for her in the church and cuts its neck with a knife."

"So Christmas dinner!" Rika said, suddenly animated.

"We borrow fancy plates from a neighbour for that meal," Nikola said.

Excitedly, Nikola went on to describe the Romani settlement under the bridge, the teetering hut where he lived with Baba, Saida and the twins, whom they were looking after. The twins never cried, but they burped, coughed and sneezed all the time. They slept in tiny pink bathtubs that Baba had adapted into cribs. Every night, Baba would sing old Romani songs to put them to sleep. After the twins fell asleep, Baba would sit by the fire and sing those same songs over and over until late in the night.

The next day at noon, Rika's truck approached Guča. Romani caravans with horses, trucks and trailers were scattered by the road. The roar of scores of brass bands filled the air.

The entrance to town was closed off by police, and only vehicles with special permission could drive in. So they had to leave the truck and the trailer and walk into town.

"It's useless to argue with the police," Almira said, fearful that Rika would get worked up. She knew how his temper could escalate. "We can drive into the fairgrounds when they open the road."

Rika approached one of the police officers directing traffic. "We came here all the way from the capital just to work at the fairgrounds. Please!"

"Do you have a parking permit?" asked the police officer.

"No."

"I can't let you in without a permit. You have to park here and walk into town."

Rika turned red with anger. "Who are those rules for anyway?"

"Provoking the police can get you to prison," the police officer said, poking Rika with his baton. "Move back!"

"He is tired, otherwise, he would never talk like that," Almira said, pushing Rika back to the trailer and handing the policeman a can of cold beer.

The police officer drank the beer down in one gulp. "It wasn't my decision, you know. I am only doing my duty, standing here in dust and traffic all day." His voice turned soft, almost apologetic.

Almira pushed Rika toward the trailer. They walked in silence.

"Well," Almira finally said, "that was a bad idea. You almost got yourself arrested." She stopped herself from adding that she had saved him. As if he didn't realise it himself.

They were stuck on the road amongst parked cars, trucks, trailers and rows of tents behind the police barricade. In the distance on the other side of the barricade, crowds of people swarmed the soccer field in between makeshift inns and bars scattered among Romani caravans. Rika parked the truck right there—on a dusty road, down the road from a gloomy inn called Bora's, which was set up in an old garage.

Rika wiped his trumpet with a handkerchief and wrapped up some bread and an onion.

"Almira, do you think you will be safe here alone all day long?"

"I think that I will manage," she said. "But do we have a choice?"

Rika checked the door to make sure it locked well. Then he wrapped his arms around Almira and kissed her lovingly. He grabbed his trumpet and waved to Nikola to follow him. They soon disappeared into the crowd that was slowly moving into Guča.

Almira climbed back into the trailer and closed the door behind her.

The downtown streets were stacked with food: grilled meat with pita bread, roasted peppers and onions, cheese pies, lamb, suckling pigs and crepes.

"Look at all the food!" Nikola said, suddenly hungry. He inhaled the sweet smell of grilled meat.

Guča was surrounded by hills, woods and mountains, and the grass smelled fresh, like the herbs Baba used for healing. The air felt clear and light to Nikola, so unlike the part of the city where he lived under the bridge. That smelled like car fumes.

"We'll eat first. I will buy you a *pleskavica*, a burger!" Rika exclaimed.

They sat on the grass at the edge of pavement to eat. "Sooo good!" Nikola cried out, gobbling it down. "Best thing I have ever eaten. Nothing compares with this."

Rika nodded in agreement.

"One of the best I have tasted myself!"

They ate in silence watching people move along the busy streets.

Rika found a comfortable spot next to Nikola. "Maybe this is a good time to tell me about Cardboard City where you live."

CHAPTER 8

Nikola's Story

NIKOLA'S GRANDFATHER HAD BEEN KILLED in a hit-and-run accident while crossing the road late one night in the thick fog of pollution that had settled down over Belgrade. He had been returning from playing trumpet in one of the crowded bars by the river.

The only witness to the accident was a homeless man who lived in a tent by the road. He ran to Cardboard City and let everyone know what he had just seen by the highway. The men from the settlement followed him to the ditch where Grandfather Alexander lay. The police came, but the case was closed due to lack of evidence.

When she heard about the accident, Baba untangled her bun and a stream of dark hair flowed heavily down her neck and spine. Baba had never cut her hair.

"My Alexander!" she screamed. And the echo of her cry reverberated in the shadow of the candlelight for hours.

Baba spoke little after the night of the accident. The rituals of mourning were well known. They were forbidden to wash or comb their hair for two weeks. All the mirrors had to be covered and they wrapped the only one they had, a broken change-room mirror thrown out by a clothing store, in Baba's scarf.

"The trumpet is not to be touched," Baba announced, placing it by the stove. "Alexander's spirit is still around. It is dangerous to upset the spirits while they are still among us."

The mourners were not supposed to eat anything but bread, water, brandy and coffee before a funeral. Every time a neighbour or friend came out of respect, Baba would weep and sigh with them over a cup of thick strong coffee.

Their silent evenings were filled with blue cigarette smoke and crumbs of dry bread. Baba wept, Saida fixed up her hair and Nikola stared at the trumpet in the candlelight, waiting for the pale fragile rays of light to fade into the evening.

• • •

There was a legendary story, which Nikola heard many times, about Gradfather's brass band performance in Guča. The band applied for the audition and played for three judges whom they took out for beer after the audition. People teased Grandfather, saying that he had bribed the judges with beer, but no one mentioned that again after the band had made it to the final night. They won fourth place. Their success was all due to Alexander, everybody agreed. His playing threw the audience into a delirium.

After their successful performance in Guča, a French record producer approached the band and asked if he could sign them up. The band returned to Belgrade as the pride of Cardboard City. The winter was extremely cold that year, but they survived by playing by the fire, warming themselves with memories of their peformance at Guča, and visions of their band on colourful record covers in French music stores.

The winter passed, but they did not hear from the French producer again. They never did go to France, but their success at Guča was told over and over. Grandfather's trumpet continued to make miracles. In freezing winter nights, the people of Cardboard City community would huddle around the fires. They would stay there for hours, motionless, wrapped up in tents, blankets and old carpets, anything they could find. It was then that Grandfather Alexander would grab his trumpet, leaving in its place a half round ring in the dust by the stove. As soon as he started playing, the shivering bundles of people by the fire would come to life. They would drop whatever they were wrapped up in and dance. Grandfather Alexander's trumpet music had momentarily lifted away their pain and hardship.

• • •

During the period of mourning, while trying to fall asleep—with water dripping through the roof onto the floor—Nikola would think about what his deda had once said: "When you turn fifteen, you will get your own trumpet."

Maybe when I turn fifteen, he thought, *I will become a great trumpet player like Deda.*

Yet, he didn't even know his own birthday.

A couple of years earlier, when Nikola was still going to school, a woman in the school office looked at his birth certificate and told him that he was nine years old. But Nikola knew she was wrong. He knew he must be older than that because it was well over a year after he was actually born that the same cousins who had signed Saida's birth certificate went to a government office to say Nikola had been born—and that they were his parents. Nikola and Saida's real mother ran away just after he was born, leaving her baby son and his older sister in the care of her parents, Baba and Deda.

With regard to knowing his age, Nikola was not an exception. Very few of the children in the settlement knew exactly how old they were. People would say: "Look how tall he is, he must be at least twelve!"

And that's how their age was determined.

• • •

"Nikolche, go to the tailor and pick up the shoes and shirts for the funeral." Baba's voice was firm, though it shook at the word *funeral*.

The tailor's hut was in the centre of Cardboard City, called the Market Place. All the businesses, such as the tailor, the hairdresser and the bar—and the church—were there. Nikola passed by the hairdresser. A young woman was sitting in the chair having her hair curled with old film containers. The Cardboard City hairdresser had a good reputation, and young Romani brides came from all parts of Belgrade to have their hair done there.

He walked into the small church and lit a candle for Deda. There was no priest, but an old woman was praying.

On the way to the tailor, Nikola passed by the bar, which was closed. It was open only on Sundays.

Nikola knocked at the tailor's, and the tailor opened the door, handing him three shirts. "Here. Tell Baba that I used my best buttons and patches to repair the shirts. They are as good as new. That will be four dinars all together."

"I like the shoes," said Nikola, pointing at the supermarket bags glued on the old shoes.

The tailor whistled proudly. "First class Italian bags. Western quality. I am saving money to go to Germany and start a business there. Take good care of them. One day they will be worth a fortune."

Nikola grabbed the shirts and handed the money to the tailor.

"I will see you at the funeral," the tailor whispered, his voice grave but sympathetic.

Back in the hut, Nikola carefully placed the shirts and the shoes beside Baba's bed. She was out and Saida was still asleep. His bed was still undone, just the way he had left it that morning, with the blanket and bedding half thrown on the floor. Nikola fell onto it, his eyes drifting toward the ceiling. Bright shards of light came in through holes in the roof.

The day didn't start well, and he was already tired. His eyelids shut heavily, and he fell fast asleep.

Nikola woke up from the smell of smoke. Baba was busy stirring something on the stove. A cloud of steam enveloped her head and shoulders. It was coming from a pot on the stove, where she was cooking the after-funeral stew. She slid the lid onto the pot and emerged from the steam as if from a cocoon. Nikola knew his Baba mostly as that misty vision of a woman hidden inside white smoke. Whether it was from smoking tobacco, cooking, or boiling herbs for her fortune-telling, Baba was seldom seen without a cloudy mist around her. It was like a part of her body.

Baba stood over Nikola's bed. Her deep dark eyes looked at him with great seriousness. "We have to start getting ready for the funeral."

"I need to find Laso," said Nikola. "I want him to come with me to the funeral."

"Yes, Laso must be there. Your deda loved that dog."

Nikola knew where to find him. All the stray dogs gathered in one place in the morning, waiting for someone to bring them the breakfast leftovers.

• • •

It was the previous winter, on New Year's Eve, when Nikola had found Laso. Winter was a particularly brutal time for the inhabitants of Cardboard City. The weather was bone-chilling cold, day and night, November to March. In sub-zero weather, they had to search for water as it froze up in the street fountains. To fight the cold, fires burned all day—the police threatened to stop them lighting fires if one more fire truck came to Cardboard City. If you sat too close to the flames, smoke stung your eyes and nose. The air inside the makeshift huts was mouldy, filled with the smell of damp clothes that never could get dry.

That New Year's Eve, Nikola had collected a load of paper he had found in schools, apartment buildings, yards, parking lots and hotels—he always made sure not to miss any place where he could find good paper or usable throwaways—hoping to sell them to buy a turkey and have it roasted in the bakery. With money left over he would buy some oranges and bananas.

He was so exhausted he could hardly feel his legs and feet. His shoes were torn, but he had found another pair in the rubbish in the alley next to the shoe store. All in all, Nikola had collected an enormous pile of paper—boxes of all kinds, wrapping paper, old Christmas cards, folders, calendars, old books, notebooks, wallpaper, maps and a pack of fortune-telling cards, which he meant to give to Baba as a New Year's gift. He had put aside hundreds of egg cartons, which were used in the walls of the huts in Cardboard City for sound insulation.

The man who bought paper from the Roma in Cardboard City came early in the morning. Nikola lit a small fire to keep warm as he waited for him to come. To stay awake, he rubbed his eyes with snow, but he fell fast asleep. When he woke up, his pile of paper was gone. Somebody had stolen it.

Nikola was shattered.

Then, he felt a warm touch on his face. A stray black dog, with white stripes on his neck, was licking the tears off Nikola's cheeks. They sat like that for a long time—Nikola crying and the dog licking his tears.

He had lost the paper, but now, perhaps, he had his very own dog—Nikola's dog—whom he would name Laso. They stayed close to each other. Laso barked at anybody who approached Nikola. He also helped Nikola find cans in the garbage, and he protected Nikola at night. Sometimes Laso slept by Nikola's side, waking him up in the morning.

• • •

"Come on, Laso. We'll be late for the funeral!" Nikola yelled when he saw Laso. The dog ran up to him holding a bone between his teeth.

"Look at you!" shouted Nikola, angrily. "You are all muddy. You can't go to Deda's funeral like that."

The dog looked at Nikola with sorrowful eyes.

Nikola picked an empty can off the ground, filled it up from a puddle and poured the water on Laso, rubbing his body. Laso shook the drops off and licked the dust off.

Together they walked back to the hut.

CHAPTER 9

Grandfather Alexander's Funeral

IT TOOK TWO HOURS TO WALK TO THE GRAVEYARD, led by Grandfather's brass band.

In the small chapel, the band played old sentimental love songs, the ones Deda performed every night working in the bar by the river. Before the casket was closed, everybody lined up to kiss Grandfather's forehead, to toss money inside and to pour beer, wine or brandy on his body.

Baba came up after everyone else. Two women walked her to the coffin. She stood there for a very long time, pouring wine into the coffin. She kept pouring and pouring, not stopping until not a drop was left. "Alexander, I poured in all my life and left it with you—in music and love, in cold and love, in sorrow and love."

Then she threw coins into Grandfather's coffin and whispered: "*Akane mukav tut le Devlesa*, Alexander—I now leave you to God."

All the people from Cardboard City lined up to throw coins in Grandfather's coffin, each whispering the same words. After they all had taken a turn at the graveside, Baba cut a piece of red string from the coffin and tied it around Nikola's wrist.

"Here is your *mulengi*, Nikolche, the string from your Deda's coffin."

"You are giving a *mulengi* to him?" said Saida. "What about me?"

She was now crying for real.

Baba continued tying the *mulengi* on Nikola's wrist.

"You can take care of yourself. We give it to the weakest one to protect him."

Ten men carried the casket to the funeral carriage, two women held Baba, and Saida and Nikola followed right behind her. The band played the funeral march, and the rest of the community followed up the steep road, avoiding muddy pot-holes and sharp rocks. Close friends and relatives walked in front, weeping.

The Romani community had been assigned their own section of the graveyard at the very back.

Grandfather's best friend, another bandleader, gave a tearful speech about his music. Then one of the gravediggers who was lowering Grandfather Alexander's casket into the grave slipped, and the casket fell to the bottom of the grave with an explosive thump. It broke apart.

Baba shouted, "My poor Alexander. Your casket broke and you threw yourself into the grave like the thunder of gods!" She stretched her arms out toward the sky, her hair spread out behind her like a dark curtain. Each one in turn threw a handful of earth onto the casket.

On the way back, Baba paid the streetcar tickets for everybody.

A smartly dressed woman complained that "Gypsies" were taking up all the seats on the streetcar. An argument ensued and the driver stopped the streetcar. "Everyone calm down or get out!" he shouted.

The well-dressed lady got off at the next stop, angrily waving at the driver with her purse. The rest of the trip went quietly, all of them gazing out the streetcar windows, absorbed in their own thoughts.

CHAPTER 10

Milos

S AIDA MET MILOS SEVERAL DAYS AFTER Grandfather
Alexander's funeral. It was a warm evening, and she had
returned home after selling flowers in restaurants. Pulling
the curtain, she entered the kitchen. Baba was sitting by the
stove, the lines around her eyes slanted upward the way they
did when she was content. Facing her sat a tall young man. He
stood up when Saida entered the room. She recognized him
as one of the students who frequented the popular cafés close
to the university library. Saida sold flowers there almost every
evening. He had kind and gentle eyes that made her feel good,
even before he introduced himself.

"He is looking for you," Baba said, pointing to the young fellow.

"Hello, my name is Milos," he said shaking Saida's hand. "I am
a sociology student and a professional photographer. You may
have seen me at the café next to the library. One of the waiters
told me that you live in Cardboard City. That gave me an idea
for a sociology project, which would also include photographs—
something about the challenges that Romani teenagers face. I
wonder if I could take some photos of you at work, while you are
selling flowers."

Saida looked at him in disbelief, standing there in their low-ceilinged hut, his neck craned forward—too tall to stand straight. Did she understand him correctly? He wanted to do a project on *her*? *Maybe I didn't get what he was saying*? she thought. He spoke like a gadjo—like the customers at the café, students and professors who argued about politics.

"I say yes," Saida said cautiously.

"Perfect," the young man said, "if it is all right with your parents."

"I have no parents," Saida said.

"Then who is your caregiver?" asked Milos.

"Caregiver? I don't need anybody to take care of me."

"I take care of them," Baba interrupted. "Saida and her brother, the orphans from my son and daughter-in-law. Their mother left them, who knows where she went."

"So, will you allow me to take pictures of Saida while she sells flowers?"

"I agree. Of course, the photos have to be respectable."

"Absolutely!" Milos nodded. "This is all above board."

He reiterated that the photos would only be of her selling flowers in the cafés. And that he would pay her for her trouble.

Then he looked at his watch and stood up to leave. "Saida, can we meet tomorrow at 7:00 at the café? I can pay for your meal as a thank you for your willingness to help. Afterward, we can start taking some pictures."

"I will try to look my best. I will put Nivea cream on my cheeks to make them look shiny," Saida said. She found Nivea cream to be the best make-up.

Milos shook his head.

"You don't have to do anything. You look fine the way you are!"

Saida still had to fetch the water from the fountain that night. But she felt that, after the young man's visit, she wasn't ready for that yet. She didn't want to think about carrying pails of water, with the cold water spilling on her toes. She earned enough money from selling flowers. She could afford to take the streetcar from first to last stop, as she did sometimes when she wanted to be alone.

The streetcar came, and it was empty. She could choose any seat, so she sat by the window. The streetcar careened down the hill by the railway station, and through the area where the city gradually turned into marshy ponds and graveyards for rusty buses and streetcars. Then it sped all the way back to the last stop, where the shortcut for Cardboard City was—between the two oak trees by the deserted fountain.

CHAPTER 11

Dinner at the Café

"I WANT TWO SAUSAGES, beans, a double burger, fries, beef soup, feta cheese and fried catfish."

Milos smiled, bewildered.

"Are you sure that you want all those dishes together? They have a long list of grilled meat and fish."

He opened the black leather menu and showed Saida the first page.

"I can't read. Moreover, I don't want to get sick from some strange food." She rubbed her hands against her skirt.

Milos stared at her.

"My hands are dirty," Saida explained.

"The washroom is right over there," Milos suggested, pointing.

On her way back from the ladies, Saida grabbed a pickle from the bar, gulping it down in one bite.

A couple of patrons at a nearby table stared at her as she sat down.

"I'm hungry. I haven't eaten since yesterday."

Milos coughed nervously. He was uncomfortable with the situation he found himself in. Since entering university, Milos had been trying to overcome his parents' middle-class prejudices. He believed passionately in social justice and equality. That's why he had chosen to study sociology, instead of what his father wanted him to study—accounting. He hoped to become an activist. This project was a step toward that goal.

"I want to work for the UN and help end world hunger," Milos said, moving the conversation toward his project and Saida's role in it.

"Well, I'm very hungry right now," Saida said. "I can't wait for the food to come. I wonder what that cook's up to? Maybe she went to the fish market to buy my catfish?"

Milos chuckled. *She might have bad manners, but she seems intelligent*, he thought, *and she has a sense of humour.*

"I'm very excited about this photography project," he said, as the food was being served.

He flicked through the photos he had already shot. *The photos are great.*

Saida started to gobble up the food. "I am starving!" she said again.

"You know what I think?"

"What?" Saida was busy sweeping up her plate with a piece of bread.

"I think that you should leave Cardboard City. You could go to school, get an education and find a job."

"I will get married and leave. My friend got married recently."

"How old are you?"

"They say that I am fifteen, but I'm older than that. Maybe sixteen or seventeen."

"Why don't you know how old you are?"

"When I was born, my mother was fifteen, and my father

was sixteen." Saida leaned back in her chair. "I want a beer."

Milos called the waiter and ordered a beer for Saida.

"So, I couldn't get a birth certificate when I was born," Saida continued, "because my parents were too young. If they went and said that I was their child, I would have been taken away into care."

"For sure."

"Some cousins finally agreed, a year or so after I was born, to sign papers saying they were my parents. I took their last name, and the date when they signed that paper . . . I don't know how it is called."

"A birth certificate."

"Yes, that's it. So the date they signed that paper became my birthday but, in fact, I am a year or more older than that. I just don't know how much."

"You have a brother who is younger?"

"Yes, Nikola. He is around thirteen, and he is often unwell. To be honest with you, who knows how much longer he will live. God forbid, he has always been sickly." Saida crossed herself three times. "We don't know exactly how old he is, because my mother ran away right after he was born, and the same cousins signed for him as for me. We were both left behind with Baba. Our cousins signed his birth certificate too, but it says he's much younger than he really is. He was a tiny baby and could barely breathe—but he survived. He went to school for a while, but not for very long. He was the biggest in the class, because they thought he was a year or two younger than he actually was. The kids teased him."

"Teased him for what?"

"Just for being Romani, of course. And for not doing well in school. He would fall asleep in class every day. The teacher had to wake him up and send him to the washroom to splash his face with cold water. Baba took him out of school, and he never learned how to read or write. Neither did I."

The waiter came over with Saida's beer, and Saida grabbed it right off the tray. She drank the beer all at once and continued with her story.

"The teacher was a good woman. She loved Nikola. She liked his singing. She often asked him to come to the front of the class and sing "Gelem, Gelem". He loves music. Nikola plays the trumpet. Like our grandfather."

"It must be difficult to live in those huts in Cardboard City."

"It gets cold in the wintertime. Sometimes, I think I would rather die during those cold winter days. People make fires with anything that's dry enough to make a fire—tires, paper and twigs."

"I can't begin to imagine all that you need to do just to survive."

"We collect paper. We beg. We sell flowers. Nikola washes car windows at traffic lights."

"Have you ever been to the movies?"

"A couple of times."

"Would you like to go again?"

"Maybe."

"How about tomorrow night? There is a good movie playing near my place. We can meet here at seven, take the remaining pictures and then go to the movies. It is my treat, a thank you for letting me take pictures of you."

"That will be nice."

"After that, I can show you my apartment. Actually, it's not my apartment. It's my parent's apartment. But I live there with them. It has a window where you can see Cardboard City."

"How will I know when it is seven o'clock?"

"At sunset then."

A group of new patrons lined up at the door of the café. Milos recognized a girl who attended one of his classes with him, waiting for a table. She was standing there, laughing, along with two boys.

Milos waved at her.

The three of them were seated at a nearby table, and the girl gestured to Milos to join them.

"I've got to go," said Saida, standing up.

A cook with pink cheeks, her white cotton cook's scarf falling over her eyes, motioned to Saida to come to the kitchen window.

"Here, take this home," she said, holding out a bag of food.

As Saida dove into the warm, moonlit August night, a street cleaner sprayed water on her feet. Saida took off her left shoe. Water dripped out of a hole in its sole like a teardrop.

CHAPTER 12

Coke with Ice

MILOS TOOK SAIDA TO THE MOVIES. The chair in the movie theatre was soft. Saida was thinking she had never sat on anything that fine and comfortable. She recalled the things she sat on in her life: stools, rusty metal and wooden chairs, streetcar seats, stairs, ground, beer cases, the pavement and grass. One time Baba found an old green couch someone had thrown out and asked some men from the settlement to bring it into their hut. But it was too big to fit inside their tiny place, so they left it outside by the entrance door. It lasted until winter when it fell apart from all the snow and rain.

The movie was in another language with Serbian subtitles, but since she couldn't read, she didn't understand what was going on. But it didn't really matter to her because she loved sitting on that soft comfortable seat and watching pretty women, fashionably dressed, flick by on the screen—with men attending to their every need.

"Did you like the movie?" asked Milos when they were out in the street.

She said yes, even though she meant the *seats* not the screen.

"Do you want to come to my place for a Coke and a snack?"

I've never been in a gadjo house before, she thought.

"I live just around the corner, only a minute from here."

He probably expects something from me, she thought. But he seemed nice enough. And he *was* handsome.

Milos lived in one of the high-rises by the river, close to Gazela Bridge—the ones with polished entrance doors and fancy stores on the street floor.

"My apartment's on the tenth floor," Milos said as they got into the elevator.

Saida followed him into the kitchen. It was all white and metallic, shiny with cooking utensils. She had never been in such a kitchen before.

"How about a cheese and ham sandwich?" he asked.

"Sure," she said.

He made the sandwiches and poured Coke into tall glasses, filled with ice. Baba didn't have fancy glasses like that, and no one had ice in Cardboard City.

Milos carried the sandwiches and Coke into the biggest room in the apartment. It had big windows looking out over Belgrade.

They sat on the couch, which was a bright yellow.

"Who's the girl in the painting?" Saida asked. The girl was smiling and playing the piano. Her demeanour, though dignified, seemed haughty.

"That's my mother," Milos said.

Saida had a bite of her ham and cheese sandwich, staring at the painting on the wall.

That woman wouldn't like to see me sitting on her fine couch with her gadjo son, she thought.

Saida put down her drink and walked over to the bookcase. It was filled with framed photos of Milos graduating from high school, Milos and his parents at the seaside, Milos at the zoo, Milos' parents dancing at a formal occasion, Milos' dad dressed in an elegant black suit.

A tall grandfather clock struck the hour.

I can't believe that I am sitting in a fancy apartment like this, Saida thought.

"Do you think that I am happy because I have a warm place to live and don't have to worry about food every minute of the day? I wish I had the freedom to make decisions on my own. This project of mine is the first thing I have done for myself. All my life I have been moving from country to country, from city to city with my father's jobs. I was in love with a girl my mother did not approve of, and she broke up our relationship. My father was entirely on my mother's side. He always will be—it doesn't matter how wrong she is. Do you see a great life here? I don't even have the freedom to fall in love with who I want. My mother still buys my clothes. Do others decide what you are going to wear?"

"This is all I have. I wear this every day. I usually wear one outfit, until it wears out or until I find something better that someone threw out."

"Sometimes, in summer," Milos said, "I walk over the bridge overlooking Cardboard City and listen to the Romani music drifting up from there. I find it very beautiful. I used to listen to one of the trumpet players in a bar by the river. His music was very powerful. He hasn't been around, so I asked what happened to him. Someone said he was run over by a hit-and-run driver."

"That was my grandfather."

"I'm so sorry."

They sat in silence for a while.

"I don't go to school," said Saida. "No one thinks of my future. No one tells me who to fall in love with. Whatever Baba cooks, that's what you get. Only one serving. When I look at the nice apartment buildings people live in, I wish I had a clean warm bed and my own room. In my dreams, there is a warm white kitchen and a fridge with lots of food inside. I never thought of myself as being free—my every day is about survival."

They sat silently again.

Saida broke the silence. "I need to pee."

"Excuse me?"

"Where do you go to pee in this place?"

Milos led Saida through the hallway and guided her to the bathroom.

This is just like in the magazines.

Colourful towels were neatly lined up on the shelf. *Even the bathroom is bigger than our hut.* Standing up, her head knocked on one of the shelves and a crystal perfume bottle fell on the floor and broke in pieces.

Saida panicked. Paralyzed with fear, she felt she had to escape. She silently opened the bathroom door and heard Milos talking on the phone.

Baba had taught her how to walk around in perfect silence. The apartment was huge, but she found the way out.

In the hallway, the door to the adjacent apartment opened and a woman with coiffured hair peeked out.

Then a man appeared. "Who are you looking for?"

Down the hallway, she found the staircase—she hurried down the tenth, ninth, eighth, seventh, sixth, fifth, fourth, third, second, and finally the ground floor. Then she stepped outside into the warm August night.

Standing on the Gazela Bridge, Saida looked down on Cardboard City. The water under the bridge had the colour of coal—visible through the rising smoke of burning tires, tall and surreal, were the tents and makeshift huts of the encampment spread out before her. She realised that was her universe.

I'll never find a place in Milos' world.

Saida felt exhausted with everything that happened and she slipped, tumbling down the iron stairs of the bridge. On the last stair, she felt a fatigue that she had never had before. She dropped to the ground and remained there for some time.

Am I dead? she asked herself, terrified by her own thoughts. She heard the stray dogs barking and knew that she was not.

A sharp pain in the rib woke her up.

"Hey! Hey!" shouted a tall police officer.

Saida leapt up, slid down the iron stairs and hid behind a giant sign. Peeking around the side, she was able to see the policeman saunter away, get into his patrol car and speed off into the morning sun.

Passing the church, the elementary school, the tower of rubbish and the myriad of boxes, umbrellas and old tents, she thought that maybe it was her destiny to live here forever. She resigned herself to a life there—the buckets, the walk to the fountain to get the water, the leaky hut, selling flowers, roaming the gloomy alleys to look for food.

It was early morning, but the heat was still suffocating.

On the way to the hut, she reflected upon the night—the movie theatre chairs, Milos' apartment, his mother's portrait with delicate fingers on the piano, the sandwiches and Coke in tall glasses with ice, the bathroom and the perfume bottle breaking into pieces, the dark water under the bridge.

Once home, she noticed that the buckets were not there, which meant that someone else had gone to get the water.

When she entered the hut, Baba attacked her with a leather belt. "What's wrong with you?" she shouted. "You were out all night! I had to go to the fountain myself. Where have you been all night?"

Baba stood above her with her hands resting on her hips. "Go and wash yourself! I made tomato soup for breakfast. After you eat, you need to go with Nikola and Spoon to collect paper."

• • •

"Do you want to hold my hand?" Spoon offered, stretching his huge bony arm toward her while she was limping behind.

Saida pushed him angrily: "Leave me alone!"

"Poor Saida," Spoon said. "Baba was really hard on you this time."

"She was away all night," said Nikola. "Baba was worried."

"I was tired and fell asleep on the stairs by the bridge."

"Baba was sorry she beat you," Nikola said.

"How do you know?"

"She poured more soup in your bowl."

"More soup? I got the same as you."

"She gave you more this time. I know because I got less this time."

"That's not true! You like it when Baba turns on me."

Saida twisted his arm. Laso jumped at Saida, barking angrily.

"Leave her alone!" protested Spoon, throwing Laso off.

"Hey, what are you doing? That's *my* dog!" shouted Nikola at Spoon.

"I am sick of all of you!" yelled Saida, limping over to a bench.

Nikola and Spoon sat beside her. Laso curled up in the shade.

"We have to hurry and get downtown before they collect the rubbish," Saida reminded them, heading toward the bridge.

"Let's catch the streetcar!" Nikola shouted.

Catching the streetcar meant getting on through the back door without buying a ticket. It also meant an opportunity to pickpocket.

"I am just riding," said Saida. "I don't want to work today."

They walked over the bridge silently, each thinking their own thoughts until they reached the streetcar stop.

They climbed aboard between elderly women in black scarves and peasants in wide flower skirts carrying baskets with eggs and corn to the market.

Nikola and Spoon sat down, not saying a word.

The streetcar turned on the curve, making screeching sounds.

"The other day," said Saida, "I almost got the wallet of a rich lady."

"And?" Nikola asked.

"She caught me by the collar and dragged me off. 'Such a young girl. Find a job and work,' the woman shouted. 'Shame on you! Why don't you work? Why don't you work?' They say that every time they see me begging on the street. Who will give me a job? Look at me now—scratches and bruises everywhere, swollen cheeks, red eyes."

Spoon just stared at the ground.

In Knez Mihajlova Street, the first coffee shops were opening, and people were already lining up in front of the bakery to buy *burek* and pogačica—rich pastry, stuffed with cheese.

"Saida," said Spoon, "zo you love me at least a bit ziz morning?" He blushed, ashamed of his speech impediment. He leaned forward to hide his embarassment.

"You smell bad," said Saida, pushing him away.

"Does Baba know that you're going out with a gadjo?" Nikola asked.

She didn't answer, and Nikola was afraid to repeat the question.

"I will wash," Spoon said and ran to the street fountain, splashing himself vigorously.

"What an idiot!" yelled Saida.

The pastry smelled wonderful, and they stopped for a moment to look at the rolls, burek and pogačica, the apple and cherry pastries in the bakery window. They wanted to eat them all.

"You don't have the money? Then close your eyes, smell and eat with your nose" was Baba's advice when they were hungry and couldn't afford to buy food. They stood in front of the window for a while, smelling the heavenly aroma of freshly baked goods.

A lady in a flowery summer dress walked out of the bakery, holding a tray with hot pogačica. They were just out of the oven, with steam rising from them.

Spoon grabbed one off the tray and sped around the corner.

"*Ludak ciganski*," shouted Saida running after him. "He is going to get us arrested."

The woman in the flowered dress shouted after them, "Lazy Gypsies! You can only steal and beg."

Saida, Nikola and Spoon hid behind a truck.

Spoon handed the stolen pastry to Saida. She started eating it right away. It was delicious and smelled like freshly baked bread. Spoon was happy watching Saida eat.

Nikola asked for a piece.

"Here," she said.

Its buttery salty taste left Nikola wanting more. His belly growled. He was so hungry he couldn't think of anything else.

CHAPTER 13

The Trumpet Festival

FARTHER DOWN THE HILL, where the main street in Guča ended and the big field started, Rika and Nikola saw long white tents set up as restaurants.

"Tonight there will be even more people out here," said Rika. "This is a small town, and nothing happens during the year. This festival is a huge thing, the only important event. You will see tonight when it starts exploding with people and music."

Rika made the sound of an explosion and laughed at his own joke.

"You will see," he said again, "the bands will roam from one tent to another—sometimes three bands in the same tent. It is called 'harmony of disharmony.' It is not perfect music. Last year a German band came, all serious educated musicians. You know what? They played very well and got applause for coming all the way from Germany to play in the local trumpet festival, but everybody knew their playing was not as good as our trumpet music—music that makes people shiver and do crazy things. Our trumpet music mustn't be perfect. What makes it so close to people's hearts is its imperfection—an occasional error, a touch of disharmony. That's what Guča's trumpet music is. That which is human can never be perfect."

Nikola nodded as if he understood.

"Anyway, back to our talk about tonight. When the guests drink a little bit, they will want the musicians to play for them the whole night. They let you know by sticking a ten dinar bill on their foreheads. You must watch people's foreheads for the bill."

"At what time does it finish?" asked Nikola

"What?"

"I mean the music at night."

Rika laughed loudly. "Hey boy, first time in Guča, so you have no idea! The music doesn't stop during the festival. There is always somebody playing. The ones who stay through the night keep asking you not to stop playing. Once, I got so tired I couldn't keep my eyes open and I told them: 'people, it's not about the money anymore, I don't care. I want to have some sleep. When are we going to stop?' You know what they said? 'When you see the sun coming up behind those hills, that's when you stop playing.' And they ordered another round of dancing, a *cochek*."

At the Zlatna Truba Hotel, Rika sat across from three Romani men who were sitting outside sipping coffee. Rika gestured to Nikola to sit down next to him. The older man was a bandleader Rika knew, a bald chubby man.

"These are my grown sons," he said, laughing, revealing a mouthful of gold teeth. "This one is around sixteen. You don't know him. His name's Tobar."

Tobar nodded.

Rika had met the older son before.

The bandleader talked on and on about the music business,

constantly rubbing his belly.

Finally, Rika called the waiter over and ordered a coffee. "What do *you* want?" he asked Nikola.

"A beer!"

Rika, the older man, his two sons and the waiter all laughed.

"A beer!" exclaimed Rika. "You are too young to drink beer. How about ice cream?"

"I want vanilla ice cream then!" Nikola shouted.

The waiter nodded and left.

Rika twisted the golden ring on his finger. "This boy here, he has a real talent for music. He only learned a bit from his grandfather and from other people here and there."

The men nodded.

"He never had a decent chance in life," the bandleader said. "I wonder what will happen to him. Do you know where he lives?"

There was a hushed silence.

"Tell them Nikola! Tell them where you live."

"In Cardboard City."

Rika nodded. "It's a settlement around the Gazela Bridge."

"I heard about that place—it's the worst," the bandleader said. "There is no basic infrastructure, no running water, no electricity. They get light from the streetlamps. They use milk cartons to build a roof and Coca-Cola crates are used as bricks. I can't even imagine how hard it is to live in a place like that."

The men nodded again and glanced sympathetically at Nikola.

The waiter brought coffee and ice cream. The ice cream was in a tall cup and had a cherry on top.

"People say terrible things about us Roma, don't they?" Tobar said.

"Yes, they say racists things. That we are lazy," called out a man with a moustache at a table nearby. "People say that we lie, that we cheat and that we steal."

Rika nodded.

Tobar played nervously with his coffee cup. "Do you know what the problem is—we need good education and good jobs."

Nikola sat still, not touching his ice cream and, as time went by, his ice cream started to melt.

"You are not eating your ice cream," Rika said. "Why? You don't like it? Take this spoon and dig into it."

Nikola brightened up and quickly grabbed the spoon as if he had just learned how to use it. He scooped a big spoonful of ice cream and stuffed it in his mouth. He soaked his fingers in the cup. He ate the ice cream and licked the bowl clean.

"Did you go to school?" the bandleader asked Nikola.

"I did but I stopped," said Nikola, licking at his fingers.

"There you go!" the man with the moustache interrupted, banging his fist against the table. "Why did you stop?"

Nikola rubbed his sticky fingers against the tablecloth."The other children teased me all the time. Nobody wanted to sit with me. I was ashamed of my lunches—bread and lard every day. I was the only one who couldn't read. One day, I ran home in the middle of class. My grandmother pulled me out. I never went back."

"See, he stopped going to school because he felt rejected," the older son said.

"One girl was nice to me. I fell in love with her for that. When she got sick and didn't come to school anymore, there was no more reason for me to go."

Everybody nodded with complete understanding.

As if to change the sad tone of the conversation, Tobar pulled a trumpet from his suitcase. "Here. You can borrow this. I can't carry this around. It's my old trumpet. I just got a new one from my uncle. You can play this one on the street and collect some change. Who knows, maybe something will pop up for you."

"You are good to play tonight," Rika said before leaving to meet up with his brass band. I will meet you here at the hotel at 11:00 tonight."

CHAPTER 14

Saida's Story: Running Away

A LMIRA TOOK THE BIG KITCHEN KNIFE they usually used to cut watermelons, wrapped it up in her shawl and stored it in her bag. It was time to fetch some water and make soup for Rika and Nikola for when they came back.

Where can I find clean water for cooking and washing? she thought.

A little way down the road she saw the sign for a restaurant called Bora's. It was the only spot lit up in the gloomy night. Hesitantly, she stepped inside. Cigarette smoke hung in the air. The tables were covered with stained tablecloths. A Romani girl in a purple cardigan with missing buttons was singing at the front. She had a long thin face, sharp chin and feverish eyes. A blonde waitress standing at the bar gave Almira an inquisitive look as she walked in, and all at once the loud and boisterous conversation that had been going on between a group of drinkers stopped dead.

Everyone stared at Almira.

"Can I help you, young lady?" the waitress asked her in a sharp voice.

She gave Almira a theatrical bow, and the place exploded with laughter.

"We parked our trailer this morning," Almira answered in a strong and confident voice. "I am looking for water. Clean water for cooking and washing."

"You can take it from the tap over there," the waitress said, pointing at the sink behind the bar. Turning to the girl in a ragged cardigan, she shouted, "Hey, why did you stop singing? Those men paid to hear you sing." She waved her hand in the air, her cheap metal bracelets clanging together.

Suddenly, Almira felt protective toward the girl. She was so thin—she looked like she hadn't eaten in days. As she went over to the sink to fill up the water bottles, she was overwhelmed by emotion. *How can I help that poor girl?* she wondered. *I could feed her and buy her a new dress.*

Almira watched the girl, who had started to sing again. She was beautiful in an unusual way. She had deep black eyes and a long nose. There was something majestic in the way she moved.

"Are you just about finished filling up your bottles, honey?" The waitress chuckled, turning to Almira. "We'll start serving breakfast soon."

"Who is the girl?"

"Oh . . . that one?" The waitress pointed at the singer. "She's just one of those Gypsy girls wandering the streets. She ran away from home. I gave her something to eat. She was starving. She can sing well, don't you think? She gets tips. And the men like her, if you know what I mean."

"What *do* you mean?"

"Are you pretending you don't understand what I mean?"

the waitress went on, raising her eyebrows. "How else can you survive if you are a young girl on the street?"

The men at the bar were still laughing, not paying any attention to the girl's sweet singing. After the waitress filled their glasses with brandy again, they became rowdy. One of them slipped off his chair. Another one pointed a finger in the air and shouted, "Stop singing!"

The girl stopped singing but stood there looking at him.

"What are you waiting for?" he asked. "For the bear to dance? No bears here!"

A wave of laughter.

"I'm waiting for my tips," the girl said in a timid voice.

"Tips? What tips? Do we owe you money for your horse?" Laughter. "You Gypsies are always begging for money."

One of the other men said, "Maybe she can earn some money another way."

"See what I mean?" whispered the waitress into Almira's ear.

"How can you allow that to happen to her?" Almira said.

"She shouldn't have run away from home. I already helped her. Without me she would be starving. If you like her so much, take her with you."

What will Rika say if I do?

"She's going with me," Almira said.

"Ask her first, honey," the waitress said.

"Come with me," she said to the girl, grabbing her hand, and together they dove out through the smoke.

Outside, the night was hot and muggy, and the air smelled of cooked cabbage and barbecued meat. Stray dogs barked in the distance and the human voices died one after another, some-where down the road. But the air was fresh and welcoming after the thick smoke inside the bar.

"What's your name?" asked Almira, as they walked back to the trailer.

"Saida," answered the girl.

CHAPTER 15

Devil Soup

"**I** AM NOT GIVING YOU THIS SWEATER. Not even to wash. I am not taking it off. It's a present from my mother."

Almira's face shone in the moonlight, undisturbed. She stood tall and strong, looking straight into Saida's eyes.

"I see, you are attached to that sweater. Fine. We can leave it aside for now. Try these things on, they don't fit me anymore. I was looking for an opportunity to donate them to somebody who needed new clothes. You are the one."

Saida didn't move or say anything, and Almira went on talking.

"I understand. You don't trust me because you had some bad experiences with people in the past. Can you try to believe me that I only want to help you? I don't want to hurt you in any way. I know that it is difficult to accept help from people, having gone through so much hardship—but please try. I can't help if you don't trust me." Almira lowered her voice and pointed at the pile of clothes. "How about this skirt and the green shirt? Green will look good on you."

Saida looked down.

Not waiting for an answer, Almira collected all her clothes and disappeared into the night. She came back with a pail of water and a soap.

"Take this and wash yourself out there. Nobody will see you—it's late and dark. When you come back, we can make dragon soup. It gives you the strength of a dragon. I learned how to cook it from my mother. She believed in the healing power of food."

"Just like Baba," said Saida softly.

"Oh, so you can talk after all. You can tell me about your grandmother while we eat. Go and wash yourself now."

Saida took the pail and soap and stepped outside.

It had been a long time since she had had a good wash like this. The splash of water, freezing cold, felt brisk against her skin.

When Saida returned to the caravan, Almira was lighting a fire in the wood stove.

"There is a nightgown on the blanket there. And I forgot to say that my name is Almira. I live with my boyfriend, whose name is Rika. We have a guest staying with us in Guča—a boy, about twelve or thirteen years old. They are at the festival now, playing. When they come back, I will have to talk to Rika about you. For now, we are making soup."

Almira put the pot on the stove and poured water in. They sat on two stools facing each other, peeling potatoes and carrots.

"Now we have to put all these vegetables in the pot," said Almira, "and let it simmer for a long time."

"Until it starts smelling like a devil," added Saida.

"You know it?"

"My Baba makes it that way all the time."

"Where is your mother, at home?" Almira asked.

"I don't know where she is, not even where she lives. I was raised by my grandmother."

Almira looked down. "I lost my mother when I was ten," she said. "Before she died, she was sick for a long time. While she was healthy, I spent a lot of time in the kitchen watching her prepare food. Sometimes, she would give me small jobs like peeling potatoes, and I remember feeling very grown up and proud of myself. That's how I learned to cook and bake."

Saida nodded. "I never met my mother. I don't even know what she looks like. Maybe I look like her. My brother, Nikola, and I never even saw a picture of our mother. I guess nobody ever took a picture of her. Baba would always get furious when she spoke about her. My mother abandoned us after my brother was born, and no one knows where she went."

"Nikola? That boy staying with us is called Nikola as well," Almira said. "What a coincidence! And your father?"

It can't be my Nikola, Saida thought. *Baba would never let him go to Guča.* "There's only one photograph of my father—a picture hanging in our kitchen," she answered. "It's covered in layers of sticky dust and fingerprints. So much so that you can't make out his face anymore. He had a dark moustache and small eyes. He died in a street fight long before we moved to Cardboard City."

"Then who took care of you when you were little?" asked Almira.

"Baba."

How is it Having a Mother?

B ABA SLEPT NEXT TO SAIDA and cooked meals for all of them. She broke nuts and watermelon into smaller pieces for Saida and Nikola when they were younger. Baba questioned Saida when she came home late and yelled at her when the chores were not done. She filled their socks with remedies made from raw potato and vinegar when they had a fever.

Girls in Cardboard City got married early and had children young. The *gadji* mothers—the ones she saw on the street, who had the money to buy ice cream and sausages—walked their children to school and taught them to give up their seats on the bus for old people. From an early age, Saida had figured out that those mothers belonged to a different world—they wore nice clothes and drove cars. They didn't have to worry about fetching water or scrounging for food for dinner.

Baba was their only family. She was the one who fed, washed, dressed and disciplined them. She was the one who protected them from stray dogs and cats when they were little. It was she who threw chestnuts at children who hurt them. Baba brought them to school on the first day, scrubbing their cheeks with her apron in front of the schoolyard. She was the one who pulled them out of school, swearing at the teachers and cursing the children who had humiliated them for being Romani and for having only bread and lard for lunch.

Other children had clean blue uniforms with collars white as snow, so sharply ironed you felt you could cut yourself by touching them. They ate soft white sandwiches with butter and ham, carefully wrapped up in tin foil, and they looked on with contempt at the bread buttered with lard that Saida and Nikola ate for lunch.

On the first day of school, nobody sat next to Nikola. The teacher, a tall woman with a neck so long that she resembled a giraffe, asked him why he was sitting alone when all the other children had partners. He said that no one wanted to sit with him.

"It's not possible," the teacher said, shaking her head. "There must be someone who will."

She turned to the class. "Who will sit with Nikola?"

They all laughed and some pretended to gag. What Nikola wanted most at that moment was to crawl into a deep hole in the ground or to run away from the long-necked teacher and the big white building full of chalk, and the children with clean hands and white collars, who ate white bread for lunch.

Then, something surprising happened—a girl raised her hand and said, "I want to sit with Nikola."

"Very well then," said the teacher, "if that is what you have decided."

She approached his desk. Her extremely thin legs hung from her short dress, and she walked like a marionette.

The class laughed. Some started teasing her, saying she was in love with the Romani boy. The girl did not pay any attention to them. She just asked Nikola which side of the desk he wanted to sit on. "My name is Zora," she said.

Zora smelled just like the flowers that Saida sometimes took from the graveyard and sold in restaurants. Zora had a treasure box of colourful erasers, sharpeners and fruit candies. Nikola never had any sharpeners or erasers. Baba sharpened Nikola's pencils with a knife.

Nikola liked to borrow erasers and sharpeners from Zora, just to have an excuse to talk to her and to look at her chestnut eyes. He fell in love with her.

Zora was the reason that Nikola went to school.

But then Zora stopped coming.

"She's very sick," his teacher said. "The whole class will visit her in the hospital."

Nikola stole some of Saida's flowers to take to Zora in the hospital, but the class never did go. At least, not while he still went to school.

One day, while Nikola was walking in the school hallway, some gadji mothers moved their children protectively away from him. He suddenly felt alone, like a strange wild plant.

Nikola ran all the way back to Cardboard City.

He rushed into the kitchen, breathless, sank his face into Baba's apron and cried for an hour. He told her all about school.

Baba was motionless while he talked. Nikola even thought for a moment that she had fallen asleep. Her knees smelled of cigarette smoke, wet soil and garlic.

When he finished his story, Baba stood up and went straight

to the school, holding Nikola's hand all the way there—cars and buses honking at them on the street. She went straight to the giraffe teacher and swore at her. She said that Nikola and Saida would not be coming back to school. Then she took Saida out of class and marched them both out of school, while those same gadji mothers watched in horror. She swore at them too. That incident marked the end of Nikola's and Saida's formal education. They never went to school again.

At first, they were relieved.

Nikola and Saida spent days playing in the dust and in the rain puddles. Saida made dollies out of plastic milk and detergent bottles. She would wrap them up nicely in old kitchen clothes and carry them everywhere she went. Lucia was the one she loved the most. Lucia was made from a large red detergent bottle. Saida used her own scarf to dress her up. She cradled Lucia to sleep at night.

One time, Saida found an old fridge abandoned by their hut. It became Saida's dollhouse. She made several other dollies and they all lived in that fridge. Nikola made cars for them out of old tin cans.

Saida dreamed about the dolls having clean white kitchens, cooking mushroom soup on the stove and making ham and butter sandwiches in soft rolls for lunch, just like the people who lived in the high-rises down the way.

Their days were filled with the fear that a social worker might appear out of the blue and take them away to one of those big buildings with windows with bars on them from which Romani orphans could never escape. Everyone knew that it was against the law to miss school, but it was difficult to track down the Cardboard City children. Their homes did not exist on any map or city plan.

A Dream Mender

W HEN SAIDA FINISHED HER STORY, Almira stayed silent for a couple of minutes and then sighed loudly.

"My life has been difficult as well, but yours is hard beyond imagination. I find that believing in a better future helps me survive."

"I find dreams help me," Saida said as she washed the peeled potatoes and placed them in the pot. "You can call me a dream mender. Each morning, I recall that night's dreams, patch them together, keep the best moments and use them to create my daydreams."

"Tell me about one of them."

"Across the street, I see the fancy windows of luxurious shops, hotels and offices. Men and women dressed up for the day start their cars and drive somewhere. The taxi drivers stand chatting in front of the hotel, waiting for the guests to come out to go somewhere exciting. I dream I will one day be one of those hotel guests heading out to a fancy restaurant."

"I would like that too," Almira agreed.

"But in real life, I just get to fetch water for our home. Or collect scraps of wood for the fire for cooking and to boil the water again to wash the dishes. Bring another pail of water to bathe the twins. Fix the laundry wire between the two roofs. Hang the clothes on the wire. Bring more water. Collect twigs to make a fire for cooking. Cook."

"How do you keep warm in winter?"

"In winter there are a dozen group fires—baby fires, old people fires, gambling fires, cooking fires. Everyone crowds up around one of the fires. Mothers try to keep their babies and young children warm underneath their shawls."

Almira got up and tasted the soup. "Hand me the salt," she said.

Saida waited till Almira had seasoned the soup before carrying on with her story.

"Even though it is dangerous, I would wait for dusk to steal electricity from the street lights. Then I would take out a brochure from the tourist bureau and try to read. Then to sleep—and dream. That's the best that I ever could hope for. If not that, then steal flowers from the graveyard and sell the stolen flowers in restaurants downtown—interrupting people while they are drinking and eating.

"Have you ever thought of returning to school?" asked Almira. "Or finding a real job?"

"Baba wanted to teach me fortune-telling, but it's all about lying to desperate people and taking their money. Baba was going to force me to get married. Or find me work as a house cleaner in a wealthy house, to wash windows and clean bathrooms. So I ran away."

"Don't you miss her?"

"I don't know, hard to say. I love her, but she is so strict. For instance, one day after Grandfather's funeral, I was sent to fetch water. To catch up with my daydreams, I took my time. Back in the hut, the feast was just ending. Two women were helping Baba clean up the table, putting empty cans and sour cream containers in the empty stew pot. I was hungry and asked one of the women if any stew was left for me. Just then, Baba came out from behind the patched curtain and scolded me for taking so much time fetching water."

Almira got up and tasted the soup again. "More garlic," she said.

Saida handed her some cloves that had been peeled, and Almira dropped them into the soup. Then she went on with her story. "I thought she'd slap me, but she just rubbed my cheek. But she said that there was no stew left for me and sent me to town to sell flowers. Still, she took care of us. She cooked us breakfast every morning, and even when there was no money, there was always something to eat. That's home for me."

"What about the twins? Whose children are the twins?"

"Baba took them in while their parents were in jail for stealing chickens from the butcher. My job was to look after them and change their diapers—made from old shirts and towels—and put them to bed. I like taking care of the twins. I like giving them a bath, drying their soft baby skin with oil, feeding them and having them fall asleep on my shoulders— holding them when they cry. It gave me confidence to be able to take care of someone else. At night, I would sing them songs and cradle them to sleep, just as I used to do with Lucia, my doll. You know what my brother Nikola once said?"

"What?"

"He said I would be a good mother. He said he would have liked to have had a mother with eyes like mine."

"Don't think about getting married. You're too young."

"My best friend got married when she was only fifteen years old. The groom was the neighbourhood bar owner, a widower much older. Five lambs and twenty-five chickens were roasted for the wedding. The music, dance and roasting went on for days and nights. The feast only ended when the police came and ordered everyone to go home."

CHAPTER 18

Angel

T HE EVENING SAIDA RAN AWAY FROM HOME, she and
Nikola had come home from their day out to find Baba
waiting for them.

"Anything today?" she asked Saida.

"Spoon stole one pogačica roll," reported Saida.

"And . . . ?"

"And I ate it whole. I gave Nikola a small piece."

"You could've given him more."

"I couldn't."

"Why?"

Saida moved forward, her body shaking. "Because I am
starving. I dream about food. I cannot think of anything else.
I don't have the money to buy new clothes, or even soap. I want
to live in a clean apartment, to smell of flower-scented shampoo
and face creams. I want to go to school and eat lunch in a real
kitchen. It doesn't seem to matter how hard I try or what I do, I
have to live in this smoky den and eat your devil goulash."

"I don't have the money to change our life here."

"You do! You are hiding it!"

Saida started searching, opening boxes and moving the

bottle crates, pulling out old clothes and scarves from the cupboard.

"It must be somewhere. I know that you are hiding the money. It must be somewhere!"

"I don't have any money. Why don't you believe me?"

"My mother must have sent you some money!"

"Your mother? Do you think she cares about you? If it was not for me, you would be dead. She left when Nikola was a baby." Baba's eyes became dark. "How dare you question me about money. I saved you. At least you're not in one of those gadjo orphanages. You know what you would become there?"

"At least I would go to school and become somebody."

"Become somebody?" Baba shouted. "The gadji teachers treated you like dirt, so you made problems for them. The gadji girls bullied you, so you attacked them and stole from them."

"None of the girls wanted to play with me because the lunches you gave me were bread and lard, bread and lard, every day."

"So? What is wrong with bread and lard? They teased you because you are Romi, you have to get used to that."

Just then Angel walked in. He was a short and stout Rom with pouting lips and tiny eyes. He was dressed in a fine suit and was wearing a colourful tie. Angel lived with his mother in a prestigious part of Belgrade in an expensive apartment. Just recently, he started visiting Cardboard City, making the rounds of different families. He had a plan.

It was rumoured that Angel had been married to a rich woman and had inherited her fortune after she died. Some people said he won big money playing poker, which he then invested in real estate—even taking part ownership in a small local bank. When he was young, Angel had been a philosopher poet, not much interested in material things. He had a Romani fiancée whom he loved very much and planned to marry. But after she left him for another man, he quit studying philosophy and decided to get rich instead.

Angel turned to Baba. "I like Saida very much," he said.

"Leave Saida alone!" Baba said, steely eyed.

"I'll give you 500 Euros, Ramina. It's a gift. And an apartment with hot water and heat. Kitchen, living room, one bedroom and a balcony. You helped me with that girl years ago—you looked in your cards and gave me good advice. I am doing it for you and Saida and Nikola."

Angel was used to getting his way.

"You have barely enough to eat," he continued. "Nikola collects cardboard day and night and is forced to beg on the street. Saida steals flowers from the graveyard to sell in restaurants. She wouldn't have to do that anymore. You will see that this is the best way. You are a fortune-teller."

"For others. Not for myself."

"You will agree in the end," Angel said as he got up to leave. "You know why? Because this is your last chance to save those children and yourself from starving before another winter comes."

"I don't believe in your deal. Where is the apartment? Tell me the address, and I will see myself."

Angel laughed. Laughing always gave him time to think when he was stuck. "It's not finished. Ramina, I assure you that I have only honest intentions. You have to learn to trust people, Ramina."

"I don't trust thieves."

"I will be back, Ramina." He left, the scent of his sweet after-shave lingering in the room.

Grandmother didn't stir from her chair, her cigarette was glued to her lips.

"I think that you should marry Angel. Why not? That can save all of us from this misery."

Saida was already at the door. "I decide who to marry, not you, Baba! I am leaving this place and taking Deda's trumpet with me."

Nikola said, "You can't take Deda's trumpet."

"Oh yes I can!"

Baba started to weep.

Saida did not waste any time. She grabbed the trumpet and ran out.

She sat squatting outside the hut in darkness, waiting for Baba to fall asleep before going any farther.

She finally heard Baba let out a deep loud sigh and say to Nikola, "Let's put the twins to sleep and go to bed."

From the shadows, Saida watched Baba close up the hut, shutting the patched curtain. Only the cars crossing the bridge broke the silence of the night.

Through the broken glass window, she could see Nikola put out the fire in the stove.

Saida drifted off into the night.

CHAPTER 19

The Performance

NIKOLA'S HAIR WAS SLICKED BACK and parted on the side—he wore a white shirt and a brown vest with oversized shoulder pads. His trousers were at least two sizes too big, and they were made of thick woollen fabric. He wore white leather loafers. That was the way Almira dressed him. He held the trumpet that Tobar had lent him, sucked up the humid river air and blew into it. It made sounds that were an entire universe of music, the most beautiful sounds he had ever created. When he stopped playing, people around him clapped in approval.

Moving heavily in his outsized clothes, Nikola approached the main stage, which was now empty. His muscles were sore. The ten-dinar bill that Baba had given him for the trip was soaking wet in his shirt pocket as he had been sweating for hours. Nikola thought about buying a cold soda but quickly rejected it as he couldn't read the menu for the drinks, and he didn't have the confidence to ask for help. *Anyway it'll be a waste of money*, he thought. *I'll just drink some water from the stream.*

Nikola sat down to rest under a chestnut tree, feeling tired.

His bones ached. He spread out on the ground and began to cry—soon falling asleep on the dried grass.

A buzzing mosquito woke him up. It was already dark and stars lit up the night sky. It felt strange to him that he was somehow free, with no one looking after him. He wasn't hungry, and he didn't have to collect cardboard. There was no one here to ask him to fill buckets with water or burn the rubbish.

And the trumpet bands clashed. Horns rang out from all directions.

Nikola dashed down the hill.

"The Roma are never shy. They can't be or they will die of hunger," Deda used to say. Instead of breaking into the crowd, pulling the shirt sleeves of wealthy-looking men and tourists, playing for them and handing out compliments while they danced, and asking for more and more dinars, Nikola stood alone on the pavement, holding the trumpet. He stood there a long time.

"Look! There's that boy with the trumpet!" a man shouted out. "He can play for us if everyone else is busy. Let's ask him."

A well-dressed family of four stood there. Two girls—one younger than him, one Saida's age. The father pulled out a bill from his pocket and handed it to one of the girls.

It must be nice to have a father who pulls out money from his pocket and hands it to you, Nikola thought.

The eldest daughter handed the money to Nikola. Her eyes shone brightly.

"Here," the teenage girl said. "Can you play for us?"

She was giving him a ten-dinar bill. *A ten-dinar bill!* Ten dinars was a lot of money. He would have had to collect paper for three nights to earn ten dinars.

"Papa, he is not playing. Do you think that he understands?"

"He may be shy."

The father came up to Nikola. His face was friendly and gentle. The wrinkles around his eyes squinted as he talked. "Won't you play something for us? All the big bands are busy for the night."

Nikola finally took the ten-dinar bill that the girl held out, folded it up and stored it with the one that Baba had given him.

He had to play now. He recalled what Baba had said about how a real trumpeter didn't ask what to play. He played what he felt. With his eyes shut, he placed his lips on the trumpet and played.

"I love that song!" shouted the younger girl.

Nikola pressed and blew, bent and curled, swayed with the sound like a cobra—then knelt and stood up again. He couldn't see whether the family liked his music or not, because he kept his eyes closed and just played.

When he finished, Nikola was silent like a caterpillar in his cocoon listening to the loud applause. A heavy hand landed on his shoulder and startled him, and there was the trumpet player whose face was on all the festival posters.

There was a crowd in front of him: blonde and red-haired tourists, women carrying bags and umbrellas, little children eating ice cream and crepes, and drunken young men with rolled-up shirt sleeves and gold necklaces with their girl friends in high heals leaning on their muscled arms.

He heard voices call out: "He is the festival champion!" "The greatest star of all time!" "He won the Golden Trumpet last year!"

And that famous trumpet player stood there looking at Nikola kindly, resting his hand on his shoulder, holding his trumpet in his other hand.

"What is your name?"

"Nikola Seich," muttered Nikola.

"The world will hear about Nikola Seich and his brass trumpet. You are very gifted. Did you know that?"

"No," answered Nikola.

"My name is Drago Nadic. I won the top prize last year. I'm in the competition this year, but tonight I decided to play on the street. I was just walking by when I heard you playing, and I was stunned to find out that you were just a boy."

Nikola didn't know what to say.

"What other songs do you know?" asked Drago.

"This is the only song I play well."

"The Roma say that 'the fox knows many things, but the hedgehog knows one big thing.' It is better to do one thing well, than many things poorly. I am sure that you can play other songs as well. Let's try this one."

So, they played. And the crowd grew, throwing more money into a box. Dancing *chocek* and *kolo*. Begging for more.

Nikola and Drago moved around, playing in the tents, at the hotel, on the street. Their fingers flew over the notes for hours.

Nikola didn't know what time it was when Drago said that he needed to sleep. He counted the money they had earned and slid some banknotes into Nikola's pocket. "Find your friends, Nikola, and get some rest. It was a long night. But I must see you tomorrow. This is the beginning of your music career. Come tomorrow at noon to the main stage and sit in front. I will be performing with my band and would like to call you up to play 'Carnival in Paris' with me. You do it so well. Do you want to play together with me on the stage?"

"I have been dreaming all my life that I might play trumpet with a brass band on the stage in Guča."

"Then we'll make sure that your dream becomes true tomorrow. Here is my card with my phone number. You can study trumpet with me."

Nikola stood there. Silent.

"You can always find me at the Golden Trumpet Hotel. I have coffee there every morning from eight to ten. If you need anything, anything at all, don't hesitate to ask. I am happy to help a young talented musician like you."

He handed the card to Nikola. On one corner of it was a golden trumpet. Then the man walked into the night.

Where was he going? He didn't remember from which direction they had come to Guča. The streets looked different than before, and nothing seemed familiar. The café where he was supposed to meet Rika was closed, and the lights of the hotel were out—only an occasional human figure meandering through the darkness.

It was too late to look for Rika. He couldn't find the way back himself and had nowhere to go. There was a statue of a man blowing a trumpet in the central square. Nikola sat on the bench underneath it, squeezing the instrument between his knees. He felt dizzy and fell asleep.

CHAPTER 20

The Reunion

THERE WAS A KNOCK ON THE METAL DOOR OF THE TRAILER. *Stray dogs*, Almira thought. She looked at the sleeping girl on the bed, her nightgown spread out. The girl seemed content.

There was a knock again, but this time she heard Rika's voice. "Open up. I need your help."

Rika was at the door, holding a boy. A Romani man, quite young, stood beside him holding three trumpets.

"We found him by the monument asleep," Rika said, carrying the boy inside.

Almira pointed to the mat on the floor.

Rika lay the boy on the mat and said, "We couldn't wake him up. He's very sick. Touch his forehead. He's burning up with fever."

I'll make my mother's remedy for fever with potatoes and vinegar, she thought. *It works every time.* She felt his forehead. *He has a high fever, very high.*

"Here," she said aloud, throwing some clean clothes on the blanket. "Take off his wet clothes."

"Who is that?" Rika asked.

"I found her in the bar while getting the water for cooking. The girl was singing there. She ran away from home and was being harassed by the drunkards."

"What are we going to do with her?" asked Rika, raising his voice.

"That's my brother!" Saida shouted, waking up. "How did he get here?"

She got up off the bed and knelt beside Nikola, touching his forehead.

"Your brother?" Almira said.

"Yes, my brother," confirmed Saida.

"Beautiful!" screamed Rika. "Until yesterday, I was just an ordinary man travelling around with his girlfriend in a trailer, making extra cash in entertainment parks. Now I have a young boy burning up in fever . . . and his sister too!"

"Rika, calm down. We have to help her out. She won't stay with us forever. And who is that young man holding the trumpets?" she asked.

"That's Tobar. I met him in Guča. He lent Nikola a trumpet. He helped me carry the sick boy. And what's your story?" he asked Saida. "Tell me the truth."

"I had a fight with my grandmother and ran away," Saida said. "I came here with my best friend, who had just got married. I figured I could get a job here. But they had a big fight. My friend ran off. Her new husband got drunk and tried to kiss me. When I refused, he pushed me out of the caravan. I got a job singing at the bar where I met Almira."

"I'll put potatoes and vinegar in his socks and rub his back with brandy," Almira said. "We can take him to the doctor tomorrow, or get some aspirin in the pharmacy."

"Nonsense," Rika said. "What is the doctor going to do? They don't know anything. And when they see Roma, they don't care."

"I know what you think about doctors, but he's very sick," Almira said.

Then she lay down to sleep, trying to find warmth under the blankets.

The first crowing of roosters cut the silence as the dawn broke. The men were snoring through Nikola's feverish breathing.

Almira fell back to sleep and when she awoke, sunlight was shining brightly through the blinds. She got up and woke Saida. The young man with the trumpets was gone, Rika with him.

Saida got up and knelt beside her brother. Her eyes were red and swollen.

Almira leaned over him. "I can't hear his breathing. What if he died?"

Almira's mother died when she was ten. She had sat for hours by her father's side during the funeral, her mother's body lying there so still, surrounded by flowers, their scent infusing the air. When it was time to close the coffin, Almira caught a glimpse of her mother's face and fainted. Someone rubbed her nose with a handkerchief soaked in vinegar. Since that day, the smell of vinegar reminded her of death.

Saida leaned over and touched the boy's head. "His fever's down."

Almira looked over at the boy. Relieved, she touched his forehead. "Yes. His fever's gone."

"Almira, you helped him recover." Saida's voice sounded different than before.

"I didn't do anything. He just got better."

"Where are those two men from last night?"

"They went to the festival," Almira answered. "They will play trumpet and earn some money."

"When I ran away from home, I took my grandfather's trumpet with me. I thought it was worth a lot of money. But when I offered it to the waitress in that bar she gave me only ten dinars."

"It's probably worth a lot more than that! A trumpet is an expensive instrument, and it should mean a lot to you as it belonged to your grandfather."

"I can't forgive myself. I wish I could get it back."

"I can lend you the ten dinars to buy it back from her," Almira said, handing her a note.

"What if she doesn't want to sell it?"

"She will."

"What if she asks for more money?"

"You can bargain. Here are a couple of coins, in case she asks for a bit more than you paid."

They headed to the bar, leaving Nikola fast asleep in the trailer.

The door to the bar was wide open, so they walked right in. There were no customers this early in the morning. Folk music blared from the radio. The place had a heavy smell of stale food, smoke and sweat.

That same blonde waitress stood behind the bar drying the dishes. She had on fresh make-up and wore white imitation pearls around her neck.

"Ohoo!" the waitress exclaimed when Saida and Almira came in. "The bird didn't fly very far. Listen, I want to make it clear right away. I don't have anything for you. Your voice is good, but you are young and inexperienced to properly entertain the guests. I can give you a piece of advice. Stick with your own people."

"I didn't come to ask for food or a job."

"Why did you come then?"

"To get my trumpet back."

"To get the trumpet back?" The waitress repeated Saida's words. "I paid you for it."

She returned to the dishes as if the topic didn't deserve any further discussion.

"I want to buy it back from you," Saida said. "I have the money."

The waitress laughed mockingly.

"Please! That trumpet was my grandfather's, and I promised it to my brother. I made a mistake in selling it to you."

The waitress's face turned softer and more friendly.

"How much do you offer?"

"Seven dinars."

"Are you crazy? I paid you ten for it. I'll tell you what. I'll sell it to you for eleven dinars."

Saida pulled eleven dinars from her pocket and handed them to the waitress.

The waitress pointed to a shelf next to the men's washroom. "It's over there. I'm glad to get rid of it anyway."

Saida grabbed the trumpet off the shelf, gagging on the heavy odour of mould and urine. She wiped the trumpet with her scarf, in a hurry to leave and never return to that place again.

Feverish Dreams

G RANDMOTHER USED TO SAY "Dreams don't tell us what will happen, they tell us what *we think* will happen." That's why it is said that only good fortune-tellers can interpret dreams.

Nikola slept another whole day through. In his feverish dreams, he was rushing through the streets of Guča in an outfit just like the one that Almira had got from the tailor. The anticipation of performing on the stage made him terribly anxious. Then the dream cut to him squeezing through a narrow alley, his trumpet stuck between the houses on either side.

From the stage, he could see men, women and children in the August heat. The sun was high, and people hid from the heat under umbrellas and festival programs, their shoes lazily resting by their bare feet. The air smelled of fresh grass, crepes and roast lamb. Everybody was waiting for something to happen, then Nikola realized that *he* was the one everyone was waiting for. But when he started playing, the trumpet flew away from his hands and disappeared in the horizon. What happened to his trumpet!

Then he saw Baba sitting on her stool, smoking and looking into the distance. A pot of devil soup was boiling, and a watermelon was rolling toward him down the stage. "Baba, what are you doing here! You must get off the stage. I am performing! You can't cook here on the stage."

Baba just sat there smoking.

"Baba!" he yelled, "you are ruining everything for me!"

"Nikolche, I will break the watermelon for you." Baba stood up and smashed the watermelon, its red juice exploding over the audience.

On the side of the stage stood Drago with his brass band looking magnificent in the sunlight.

My trumpet has flown away. Now, how am I going to play?

A tiny girl came onto the stage from the audience. He recognized Saida's green sweater with the missing buttons. She handed him Deda's trumpet.

"This is the moment," Drago announced, "to introduce my young friend Nikola Seich. He plays trumpet the way I have never heard it before."

And they played together.

When they finished playing, the crowd carried them on their shoulders. The air was dry, and it was so hot that the heat had melted drink cans into the asphalt.

Nikola sat on a wall and his feet were wet and his shoes felt as if he had rocks in his socks.

In the early evening, Nikola woke up to the aroma of devil stew. He sat up and yawned.

"Nikolche, you are awake. Thank God you are better. The fever is gone," Saida said, touching her brother's head. Her swollen eyes brightened up. "Your forehead is cool now."

Saida crossed herself three times and dried up her tears with a handkerchief. "I was so worried about you, Nikola. You had a bad fever. I thought that if you did survive, I wouldn't get angry with you ever again." She smiled. "You are finally breathing normally."

Almira stood behind Saida, holding a jar of water. "Here, drink some water. You were sweating a lot. You must be hungry now that you are feeling better."

Just then Rika stepped into the trailer. "I could smell that soup from down the road," he said. "Smells like devil soup!"

Nikola sat up. "Am I dreaming? Is that you, Saida?"

Saida nodded, unable to speak, and hugged her brother. They both started to cry.

Nikola jumped up. "I have to run. A man named Drago is waiting for me by the main stage at noon today."

"That must have been yesterday," Saida said. "You were so ill you slept through the entire day."

"I found you sleeping under the monument," Rika said. "You were burning with fever when I brought you here." After a moment he asked. "How do you know Drago?"

"I met him at the festival. He gave me his card with his name and phone number. He said to meet him by the festival stage at noon. He said I could play with his band. I put his card and the money I earned in the back pocket of my pants."

"We had to change your clothes," Almira said calmly.

"You were sick with fever," Saida said. "We rubbed you with *rakija*, vinegar and my herbs. I washed your pants and shirt, but I didn't find a card or any money there."

Nikola started to cry. "I have to go and find him."

"Nikolche, Nikolche, don't cry!" said Saida, handing him the trumpet. "Here! Look what I have: Deda's trumpet. It belongs to you, now."

Almira interrupted. "The soup is ready. I think that we should eat. Then you need to sleep. Regain your strength."

Nikola brightened. "Drago said he goes for coffee every morning at the Zlatna Truba Hotel."

"Early tomorrow morning I'll go and find him for you," Rika said.

Rika, Almira and Saida ate hungrily, concentrating on their food. When they finished, they saw Nikola fast asleep, his untouched soup on the table in front of him, his head resting on Grandfather's trumpet.

CHAPTER 22

Talks and Reflections

WHY AM I DOING THIS? I must be out of my mind. Haven't we already done enough for those two? Fine. People must take care of each other. We thought that he was dying, and his grandmother left him in my care. But there is his sister as well, who Almira decided to save from walking the streets. Another person to share our trailer! Anybody else? Maybe we can take in more people off the street and share our stew with them. I met up with Drago Nadic for him. That's enough charity work for me.

Heading back to the trailer, Rika let his thoughts run on. He had met Drago at the Golden Trumpet Hotel and explained what had happened to Nikola. Drago said that Nikola was gifted, and that he could help him develop his talent. *Well, whose accomplishment was all that? It was me, Rika. I brought that boy to Guča. It was my doing that he got to borrow that trumpet from Tobar. I took care of the boy when he got sick, well . . . Almira did, but that's the same. The boy will be over the moon when he hears about my meeting with Drago.*

A strange boy, fragile and sensitive. Rika had never seen

such a serious twelve-year-old. *He has a talent for music. He plays that song 'Carnival in Paris' well.*

Feeling good about himself, he stepped in the caravan.

Almira and Saida sat on the stools, cutting vegetables and whispering. Nikola was awake, huddled in the corner holding the trumpet.

"Where did he get the trumpet?" Rika asked Almira.

"It's my grandfather's trumpet," Saida said. "I took it when I ran away from home."

"Nikola, I went to the Zlatna Truba Hotel and met Drago. I explained everything." He handed Nikola Drago's card. "He gave me his card and said you could contact him. He wants to help you. He believes you are a very talented musician."

Nikola's cheeks blushed and looked feverish. "Are you sure that he wasn't angry?"

"Why would he be angry?"

"He told me that we could play together on stage, and I didn't go."

"I explained that you were very sick," Rika said.

"You were barely conscious," Almira added.

"We were worried that you wouldn't survive," Saida added, reaching for her brother's hand.

"Thank God you are better now," Almira said. "Otherwise I don't know how I would face your grandmother, returning with a corpse instead of bringing back her grandson."

"Drago still wants to see you," Rika stressed. "He said: 'tell Nikola that he can come to my home in Guča anytime he wants to study trumpet with me. I will help him become a real musician.'"

A little exaggeration won't hurt, Rika thought.

Nikola threw himself on the floor and embraced Rika's knees. "I am so grateful for everything you have done for me. I will never forget you."

Rika was uncomfortable. The boy's reaction was unexpected. He was fine when cheating, gambling or playing the trumpet for money. He liked doing good deeds and getting a small reward for that, and it certainly felt good when somebody thanked him, but *this* was too much. Yet, it was true, he couldn't remember when he had done this much for anyone. He didn't know how to respond to such gratitude.

"Nikola, what's the matter with you? Get up!" he said.

That evening, by the time Rika returned from the last day of the festival, Nikola had recovered fully.

"Almira, let's eat soon! We have to wake up early tomorrow and get ready for the trip back. I will collect some branches for the fire. Do you want to help me, Nikola? You need fresh air."

He pulled the boy up and hurried him through the door.

It was drizzling and Rika took off his hat to cover Nikola's head.

They collected fallen branches for the fire.

They all sat around the fire. Nikola played Deda's trumpet and Saida sang. They told stories about Baba, Spoon, their hut and the paper collecting. Almira found it difficult to believe their stories about life in Cardboard City. She had passed the settlement under the Gazela Bridge so many times but had never thought much about it. She knew Romani people lived there, but their lives did not seem real to her.

It's almost as if those people live in another reality, Almira thought. *They live in an alternate world under that bridge.*

She realized that while they didn't have enough food, money and the comforts of home, they tried to replace what was missing as best they could with music, dance, stories, laughter and magic. Almira came to understand that their lives—with their own laws, customs and values—though laced with sorrow, were rich with dreams.

Listening raptly to Nikola and Saida's stories, Almira thought, *They're beyond human. They're like saints.*

CHAPTER 23

The Ace of Hearts

Almira found Baba's hut in Cardboard City by following the directions from the map that Rika had drawn based on Saida's instructions. She recognized it by the umbrella on top of the roof. She came up to it just as Baba was telling fortunes. Almira decided to hide in the bushes and wait.

It had been several weeks since Saida had confided in her that she couldn't return to the homeless settlement under the bridge and the life of misery she had lived before she met Almira and Rika.

"If I go back there," she said, "I will never get out. I will be hungry and cold for the rest of my life."

Almira asked Rika what he thought. Maybe they could take in both of them. The summer was ending, and they were going back home. The apartment that Rika had inherited from his grandfather was spacious enough for four people, and he earned enough in his regular job as a mechanic. They could help Nikola and Saida get all the documents they needed to register their residence at their place and start going to school. Considering that they were orphans and Ramina was practically homeless with no income, Almira had hoped it wouldn't be difficult to obtain guardianship of Nikola and Saida. They found out that they could apply for help from the government as well. All that would take time, but Nikola and Saida could stay with them while it was being sorted out.

It was time to talk to Baba.

Almira arrived at the settlement confident and determined. She would first say what she had planned to say and then negotiate with Ramina. Yet, seeing Baba through the small window, Almira was suddenly overwhelmed by fear of the old woman's reaction.

Is she going to be relieved to hear that her grandchildren will have a chance to live better lives? Or will she be angry and try to stop them leaving?

• • •

"Ace of hearts. Good. Home and love. Pleasant news. Love letter. Watch out for gossip."

Baba dropped the cards and lit up a cigarette. "I'm not saying anything else. You only paid for a short fortune-telling."

The woman slid a note into Baba's pocket, satisfied.

An elderly woman entered the kitchen and sat down across from Baba. "I haven't heard from my husband for three days. I don't know what to do. Something bad may have happened to him. Maybe he left me. Can you find out in your cards?"

"Of course! Who around here is a better fortune-teller?"

The woman wiped her eyes with a pink handkerchief. "I am so worried, Ramina. I haven't slept for two days."

Baba laid out the cards. Three rows of seven cards, from left to right. The woman sat still, rigid with anticipation.

Baba opened the cards. Ten of spades. Not good, She didn't like to be the bearer of bad news. "The future is not clear. Happens when the weather is not stable, the stars don't show up properly."

"What do they say?" the woman insisted. Her face was white and the dark bags under her eyes trembled.

Baba mixed up the cards. "I already said that the future is not clear."

The woman stood up and stormed out angrily.

Almira knelt in the bushes trying hard not to make a sound. She suddenly had doubts, and empathized with the woman. She must care deeply for Nikola and Saida, and she didn't know where they were. She must be wondering if they were alive and well, or if she would ever see them again? She must be wondering what could she do to get them back.

I'm hiding two steps from her table, and I have all the answers, Almira thought.

Baba laid out the cards, whispering to herself, "For Saida, first. Queen of clubs, young friendly woman. Who is that young friendly woman? What about Nikola? Ten of clubs, successful journey; Nine of spades: unexpected good luck. What is this card saying? Sickness. Luck. He was sick but got better."

I shouldn't look into my own future. But I have to find out what is happening to the children. Loss of money and tears.

It must be the money I lost to Angel. She thought about his real estate office and the crowd of people standing outside, shouting that they had been cheated.

Baba had lost all her money saved during her many years of collecting paper, doing fortune-telling, cleaning people's houses, selling plastic bags, lavender and vegetables at the market–it was all gone.

Angel had shut down his office and ran away with all their money—probably to Argentina. The police were looking for him. It turned out that Angel sold fictitious apartments for a small down payment. Attracted by what had seemed like a good deal, Angel's clients lost everything they had.

Laso started to bark, and there was a knock at the door. Almira entered through the narrow curtain opening.

"Good afternoon," Almira said. "I am sure that you remember me."

Baba didn't bother to answer the question. She waited for Almira to continue.

"It's about Nikola. He got very sick in Guča with a fever, after playing for hours with a trumpet master called Drago. He heard Nikola playing on the street."

"I thought I could trust you to keep him safe!"

"He's better now." Almira was on the verge of tears. Her self-confidence had vanished. "We waited for him to get better before coming back. It took him time to recover."

"Where is he now? Oh, Nikolche, Nikolche!"

"I am sorry to be getting back to you so late. I know you expected us to be back with Nikola after the festival was over."

"Where is he?"

Almira's eyebrows trembled. Since childhood, it was something that happened to her every time somebody yelled at her.

Baba's voice had the power of thunder. Her head dropped in her lap and it seemed as if the length of her dark hair filled up the room.

"I have good news for you. Saida is here," Almira said. "She is waiting for me in our truck. It was an unbelievable coincidence. I met her in Guča. She was working in a bar. We invited her to stay with us. The two of them are reunited. A miracle, isn't it?"

"Where is the truck?" Grandmother said, staring at Almira with her dark eyes.

Almira was startled by the old woman's dark eyes, and she stood frozen to the ground. Struck by the burden of hardship in those eyes, she led her to the truck.

Saida sat in the truck watching the cars stuck in rush hour traffic. Rika was trying to find a folk music radio station. He handed Saida an apple. She took it from him looking at her own hands, now soft and clean. In the last couple of weeks, Saida discovered the new pleasures: daily baths, hand creams, deodorants and healthy food. Saida was confident she made the right decision to run away. Now, maybe, a new life awaited her. Picturing herself sleeping in that cold, half-open hut in the winter rain, with an empty stomach, made her determined never to go back. She begged Almira and Rika to keep her and Nikola with them and somehow, miraculously, they agreed. Nikola said now that he had Deda's trumpet, he would be able to make his way in the world. Nonetheless, Saida despaired about Baba sitting in the hut lonely, holding coffee between her two bony fingers.

When they approached the settlement, they all knew that Saida and Nikola couldn't return there: the fierce stench of garbage and burned tires, children playing with frogs in puddles.

I won't miss the smell of garbage and burned tires, she thought.

A loud crack of thunder brought her back to reality. Stray dogs barked. And there was Baba pounding at the door of the truck, her eyes burning with rage.

Saida stepped out, afraid. Rika followed.

"Where have you been? I almost died of worry and grief. You ran away and took Deda's trumpet. No one knew whether you were alive or dead."

Baba lifted her arm to strike Saida, but Almira stepped between them.

"I know how much you care about me, Baba," Saida said trembling, suddenly feeling very weak. "You waited for me desperately, you worried. I know you missed me. I know how much you suffered."

"I raised you after your parents were gone. You are my child."

"I know, Baba, but you couldn't give me a proper home—a real family."

"What is a *real* family? A family is a family, people who live together and share the pain of life. That's what it is. I don't know what else I could do to make it *real* for you. I made our hut our home. I fed you. I never left you. I made you dolls, and I protected you from stray dogs."

"I want to have a real home, not one with leaky roofs made from umbrellas—a place without smoke burning my eyes and wild dogs barking through the night. I want to go to school and learn how to read. I don't want to live here ever again."

"Rika and I discussed it," Almira broke in. "We can keep the children at our place. They'll be safe, well fed, and go to school. We are here to tell you that Saida and Nikola are going to live with us. This is not the place to raise children and you know that yourself. You can't even meet their basic needs—they are hungry, cold and unsafe here. They don't go to school. They have no future if they stay here."

"You can't take my family away! Saida and Nikola are all I have."

"They will still visit you," Almira said. "We won't be far away."

"And you have the twins," Saida said.

"We live like this because I was unable to get a real job. People here don't care about us. We are invisible to them. Roma women can't get jobs. I can just do fortune-telling or collect paper. You are a gadjo, the entire world is made for you. And why Nikola? Does he hate it here as well?"

"All he cares about is his music," Saida said. "His dream is to study trumpet and become a famous musician. Almira and Rika will help him with that."

"Rika and Almira? Are they already your family! You think that they can really accept you as their own?"

"Ramina . . . " Almira's voice turned cold. She wanted to get it over with. "No one is taking your children away from you," Almira said. "We are just offering a better place for them to live. We can be their guardians until they turn eighteen. We have a big apartment. What do you say?"

"Then take them with you! Go!" Baba turned to Saida. "You too! Go away with your new family and don't come to me ever again, none of you," she wailed.

Saida quickly jumped in the back seat, but when the truck

started moving, she just had to turn and look back one more time.

Baba was walking back to the hut, surrounded by stray dogs.

CHAPTER 24

A Gift for Goodbye

RIKA DROVE SLOWLY TOWARD THE BRIDGE. "Stop!" Saida broke the silence. Spoon was standing by the side of the road, and she had a gift for him.

Reaching into the pocket of her dress, Saida took out a small package wrapped up in old newspaper.

"Spoon, I brought you a present."

"What is it?" Spoon rarely got any presents. "Something to eat? A pogačica from Guča?" The fact that Saida brought him a gift was a miracle in itself. The girl he loved was handing him a present! Was there anything better he could expect from life?

"Stop guessing. Just open it," Saida said in a firm but gentle tone of voice. "Be careful, don't break it."

A stream of sunlight shot through the trees as Spoon ripped off the newspaper wrapping.

"I found a pair of glasses on the street in Guča and thought they might help you to see better. Try them on. They look new."

He tried them on.

"What do you think? Can you see better?"

"Sure," said Spoon, trying to sound excited. He couldn't see a thing. "Much better! I can't believe that I finally have glasses.

My stupid eye! So tell me, Saida . . . you saw the glasses and thought about me?"

"You are the only person I know who needs glasses."

"You could've sold them."

"I know. But I wanted you to have them."

Spoon stood there, feeling weak and abandoned, uncomfortable with his new glasses, their lenses reflecting the sunlight.

Saida embraced him affectionately. "Spoon, I know that this will be sad news for you, but I have to tell you I came to say goodbye. Many things happened during the time we were away. Nikola and I realized that we wanted to go to school, and we understood how much we needed to stick together. We met some good people, and they agreed to take care of us. They're in the truck."

"What does that mean?"

"That means that they will sign some papers and we will be like a family. We will have a real home."

"What was wrong with your home here?"

"Well, it's not really a home. It's more like living on the street than a home."

"But . . . does it mean that I won't see you anymore?"

"I will come to visit. Nikola too," she whispered as Nikola stepped out of the truck to say goodbye to his friend. "You'll always be special to me, Spoon."

"Goodbye my friend," Nikola said, tears falling from his eyes.

Spoon grabbed Saida's hand and squeezed it hard.

CHAPTER 25

Delivered by Hand

Belgrade the 19th of January, 2007

DELIVERED BY HAND
Ms. Ramina Saich
(Address unknown)
Dear Ms. Saich,
RE: Assigned Guardianship
     Minors: Nikola Saich and Saida Saich
     Our File No.: 03-1674

This letter is to inform you that we have received your duly endorsed documents with respect to the guardianship of your grandchildren SAIDA SAICH and NIKOLA SAICH.

You will be informed about the next level in this process in due course.

We appreciate your cooperation in this matter and trust that you will not take any steps contrary to the Guardianship Agreement dated January 10, 2007.

Please feel free to contact the writer, should you have any questions or concerns.

Sincerely,

Milos Domich, Social Worker
MINISTRY OF SOCIAL SERVICES, REPUBLIC OF SERBIA

March 7, 2008

Dear Nikola,

My name is Lydia and I am involved in the Family Connection Project. We help families who are separated to stay connected by correspondance. As I understand it, your grandmother still lives in the settlement in Belgrade, while you and your sister have moved in with your guardians. If you wish, you can write a letter to your grandmother and I will take it when I visit her, read it to her, and write down her answer to you.

Sincerely Yours,

Lydia

April 1, 2008

Dear Lydia,

I was so happy to get your letter.

In this envelope, I included a letter for Grandmother, extra paper, stamps, and envelopes for her letters and a small chocolate for her. She'll be surprised that I can write. There is also a small chocolate for you.

Saida

Dear Baba,

I dreamed of you again! You tried to break the watermelon in my school and the principal asked you to leave. I wasn't angry, just happy to be with you again.

I miss you.

This letter I am writing by myself. I learned to write. Every day I go to school. I am never hungry and I am learning to read and write music. One day I will play trumpet like a real musician.

Everyone tells me that I have a "gift" for music but I don't understand how. Gifts are those things we give to someone special and when we have extra money. That's what I thought "gift" meant? I live much better now but I would like you to be here as well.

How are you? Do you have enough coffee and brandy? We will bring some when we visit soon.

Saida is sending you hugs and kisses. She will write you soon herself.

How are the twins?

Love

Nikola

May 30, 2008

Dear Nikola,

Thanks for the chocolate.

Your grandmother is proud of you. She asked me to read your letter over and over, and she keeps it now inside her blouse. Here is what she dictated to me for you.

Lydia

Dear Nikolche and Saida,

I don't trust this girl's writing and I don't have much to say.

Nikolche, I will come to your dreams every night, and I won't make any trouble there.

It's good that you have enough food, you are so thin and weak.

I have brandy and coffee, but I miss you both. This hut is now a place of sorrow when you are not there.

My bones hurt a lot. I am getting very old. Everything else is good.

God bless you!

Baba

September 10, 2008

Dear Lydia,

I wrote a letter for Baba. It took me some time; I am still not so quick in writing. Would it be possible to get this letter to Baba? We are so fortunate to have you do this for us.

Saida

Dear Baba,

I wanted to show you that I learned to write and read as well not only Nikola. We both go to school now. It's fine but I don't have any friends. I must go to a special school because I am many years behind. At least I can read the signs on the street and the magazines. When I finish this school I want to work in a flower shop.

We are happy here. We have enough to eat and we sleep in a real bed.

Almira promised to bring you one day to visit us.

Saida

December 15, 2008

Dear Nikola,

This winter has been hard in Cardboard City. Grandmother has problems walking and she coughs. Probably, because she smokes a lot.

Here is what she asked me to write.

Lydia

Dear Nikolche,

The fortune-telling is not going well, and I can't move fast enough to collect paper. I sit in the hut by the fire almost all day. Luckily, I don't need much.

It's good that you and Saida are not here in this cold weather.

Baba

January 10, 2009

Dear Baba,

We hope that they will find a home for everybody in Cardboard. We heard people saying they will move everyone from Cardboard City. They want to build a hotel out there. Then you will have a warm room and a bathroom to wash your hair. We are sending you some money to buy something good to eat.

Nikola wrote some music for trumpet, and we recorded it on a tape for you to hear.

Ask someone to play it for you. You will like it.

Nikola and Saida

June 4, 2009

Dear Saida and Nikola,

I am sorry for such a long gap in our correspondence. I was busy with other projects and the organization did not have anyone else to replace me.

I went to Cardboard City yesterday and was surprised to find only a huge hole on the spot where the slum used to be. It's all gone. There was no trace of your hut, only a big puddle in that place.

Most of the settlement was moved to some barracks on the outskirts of Belgrade. They say that people complain about being far from the city centre where they can't collect paper or find jobs.

I am sorry that we lost connection with Grandmother.

I will write you once I know more.

All the best,

Lydia

September 2009

Dear Nikola and Saida,

Do you remember me? My name is Marijana. My mother was your grandmother's neighbour in Cardboard City. They moved together to Surčin—the new complex built for the people in the settlement. We shared a barrack with Ramina.

My mother asked me to write you this letter, since she can't read or write.

Ramina kept all your letters in her special tin box. She had been waiting for the new one in the last few months of her life. That, in fact, was everything she hoped for. Her legs got so bad that she couldn't move anymore. She spent the last week lying in bed and smoking. She even stopped drinking coffee. My mother knew that she wouldn't last long. When Ramina died, Mom collected all your letters, her coffee cup and her lighter and made this package for you. I found this address on one of your letters. (I hope it is still the same). I also hope that I am not the first one to break the sad news to you.

At least, you have a little something to remember your grandmother. The letters, which she kept inside her blouse for a long time before placing them in the box—still carry her scent.

RAMINA'S DEVIL STEW

Fry 1kg of beef stew meat, 2–3 fresh chopped peppers and 2 chopped onions in vegetable oil. Add minced garlic, salt and black pepper, 2 cups water and 2 teaspoons powdered paprika. Bring to a boil, then simmer on minimum heat for 2 hours. Keep adding water and powdered paprika in small amounts as needed.

In a bowl, mix 1 cup of flour, a teaspoon of baking powder and 1 cup of breadcrumbs. Mix well. Add water until you get a thick paste. Make small balls of dumplings and drop them into a pot of boiling water. Cook until they swell and float to the top.

Remove the dumplings and let them cool in the open air. Serve the stew in the same pot it was cooking in for everybody to share. Use the dumplings to spoon up the stew from the pot.

SECRET MUD KACAMAK

Wrap corn flour in a plastic bag and place inside a tin box. Dig a hole in the mud and cover the tin box to protect the corn flour from mice and insects.

Boil 1L of water with as much salt as your thumb and index finger can hold. Keep adding the corn flour you have retrieved from the mud until you get a thick soup.

Add butter, lard, oil, or margarine. Keep stirring.

Serve extra hot with feta cheese, sour cream or plum jam.

SERBIAN CORN BREAD (PROYA)

In a large bowl, mix 5 cups of cornmeal, 1 teaspoon salt, 1 cup butter or margarine, 3 beaten eggs and 2 cups milk. Pour into an oiled baking pan. Heat oven to 380 F and bake for 60 minutes or until the crust is brown and crispy. Cut into squares and serve with kaymak (clotted cream).

POPARA (BREAD PORRIDGE)

Ingredients:

2 cups water

1 cup milk

5–6 slices day-old bread

2 tablespoons butter, lard or margarine

1–2 cups feta cheese

½ spoon salt

In a saucepan, bring to boil the water, milk, salt and butter or lard. Break or cut bread in small pieces and drop into the boiling mixture. Stir until the mixture starts to thicken. Add the cheese and serve hot.

EPILOGUE

In May 2009 the Government of Serbia decided to displace the families from Cardboard City within 45 days.

The families coming from other provinces were returned to the places they came from, and they became the responsibility of the government. The families residing in Belgrade (122 of them) were temporarily placed in shipping container homes. The families had the right to receive social assistance if their children attended school.

On August 31, 2009, Cardboard City was cleared, and all the Roma families were resettled in five Belgrade municipalities, or returned to the towns of their former residency.

HISTORICAL NOTE

Historically, the Romani people—or the Roma as they are usually referred to—have been severely persecuted and marginalized, particularly in Central and Eastern Europe where the vast majority reside. The profound discrimination and virilant racism they experienced culminated in the *Samudaripe*—the genocide of Europe's Roma population at the hands of the Nazis during the Second World War. Some 500,000 Roma were deported and killed during this period.

Even today, numerous laws and coercive measures against this community—in a number of Central and Eastern European countries— serve to perpetuate well-entrenched anti-Roma racism. Romani people are often trapped in extreme poverty owing to the structures created by the dominant culture, which—as is shown in Jovanovic's *Cardboard City*—erects near insurmountable barriers to their integration into society. Romani settlements are routinely subjected to frequent demolition, causing the routine uprooting of communities.

The Roma are often forced to live in the inhumane conditions depicted in the novel, without the social, economic and educational opportunities available to the wider society. This struggle for survival and the reality of persecution has historically forced the Roma to move long distances from one country to another, creating a cycle of migration, born out of the necessity to survive which continues up to the present day.

Dr Hedina Tahirović-Sijerčić

Dr Hedina Tahirović-Sijerčić is the author of *Romani čhib: An Overview of the Romani Language and Culture* and the autobiographical novella, *Rom Like Thunder*. She is also the co-editor—with Cynthia Levine-Rasky—and a contributing author of *A Romani Women's Anthology: Spectrum of the Blue Water*. Hedina published six children's books and several collections of poetry as well.

The fictional story of Nikola, Saida, Baba, Almira, and Rika—and the inhabitants of Cardboard City—was taken from a novel written by the author in Serbian called *Kartonac*, published in Belgrade in 2019.

LIBRARY AND ARCHIVES CANADA CATALOGUING IN PUBLICATION

Library and Archives Canada Cataloguing in Publication
Title: Cardboard city / Katarina Jovanovic.
Names: Jovanovic, Katarina, 1962- author.
Identifiers: Canadiana (print) 20230131956 | Canadiana (ebook) 20230132375 | ISBN 9781990598104 (softcover) | ISBN 9781990598111 (EPUB)
Classification: LCC PS8619.O86 C37 2023 | DDC jc813/.6—dc23

Book design by Elisa Gutiérrez

The text is set in Georgia Pro. Titles are set in Source Sans Pro.

10 9 8 7 6 5 4 3 2 1

Printed and bound in Canada on ancient-forest-friendly paper.

MIX
Paper from responsible sources
FSC® C016245

The publisher thanks the Government of Canada, the Canada Council for the Arts and Livres Canada Books for their financial support. We also thank the Government of the Province of British Columbia for the financial support we have received through the Book Publishing Tax Credit program and the British Columbia Arts Council.

BRITISH COLUMBIA ARTS COUNCIL
An agency of the Province of British Columbia

BRITISH COLUMBIA
Supported by the Province of British Columbia

Canada Council for the Arts   Conseil des Arts du Canada

Canadä